Strange Weather

Strange Weather

BECKY HAGENSTON

Press 53 . Winston-Salem

Press 53
PO Box 30314
Winston-Salem, NC 27130

First Edition

Cover and interior design by Erin T. Dodge

Library of Congress Control Number: 2010903070

Printed on Acid-Free Paper
ISBN 978-0-9825760-7-6

For my sister, who has weathered plenty of strangeness with me

Contents

Strange Weather

Trafalgar

On their first day in London, the papers are full of stories about people freezing to death all over England. A couple from Kent drowned when they tried to rescue their dog (it lived) from a frozen pond. There's a picture of the dog, a damp and panting Irish setter, on the front page of the *Daily Mail*. "The Dog That Cost Two Lives," says the headline.

"I should save this," Julie's mother says, "so we can prove to your father that England is not always *temperate*." They are in a pub across the street from their bed and breakfast, in Belsize Park. Outside, the sky is as thick and dreary as Julie had hoped it would be, fat flakes swarming in the air. She's drinking her second pint of cider and feels pleasantly dizzy. She says, "Yeah, let's prove just how cold it was." Julie's lover, Henry, had said the same thing, that winters were mild and it never snowed.

Henry is supposed to be sitting across from her right now. He's the one who told her they would come to this pub, where he used to drink years ago when he was studying abroad. "I was getting drunk in pubs when you were in the womb," he told her. This is the sort of thing he says often. When I was here, you were here; when I was getting married, you were getting your first teeth, as if drawing some invisible line through time, connecting them.

He'd said, "I can't wait to have a drink with you in the King George." The pub is almost empty; a jukebox is playing music that was popular ten years ago, and the barmaid, a gaunt, red-haired girl, is drinking something that looks like rum. After a drink at the King George,

Henry had told her, they would go to Trafalgar Square and look at the Christmas tree. "On New Year's Eve we could go there if you want," he said, in a voice that made it clear that he disapproved of this idea, and would disapprove of her wanting to go.

Then there was also the matter of his job, his research, the reason for this whole trip. He was writing another book on English painters—Pre-Raphaelite this time—and would be spending much of the week in libraries and galleries. Julie would spend these days exploring on her own; she had made a list of the places he said she should go, interesting things to see. "It'll work out well," he said, "since I've done all that touristy business before. You can see the sights and then we'll meet back at the hotel in the evening and go to the pubs."

She had imagined them rushing through dark, rainy streets together, and riding on double-decker buses. She had imagined them standing in swirling snow, on Tower Bridge. ("It doesn't really get cold enough to snow in the city," he'd said, but here it was, snowing, as cold as it was back in Pennsylvania.) But the snow wasn't even important; what was important was being far away from anyone who might know them, where they could just be any couple, any happy couple anywhere.

Julie looks across the table at her mother, who is letting her tea get cold and examining her plane ticket with a frown.

"You're not ready to go home already, are you?" Julie says, and her mother shakes her head.

"I'm just trying to make it seem real, I guess." Her face is flushed. She looks, Julie thinks, almost embarrassed. "I'm just trying to get it through my thick skull that I actually flew across the ocean." She looks at Julie. "With you," she says.

%

Julie's mother, Ann, has a powerful, irrational fear of flying. She knows it's irrational because she's never been in any sort of accident, or even turbulence; no one she knows has ever crashed or come close to crashing; she is aware of all the statistics about how flying is safer than driving a car.

It has something to do with feeling out of control, at least that's what she's read in certain books on the subject. Her husband, Richard, is a psychologist, and that's what he thinks, too. He gave her a relaxation tape to listen to on the plane, but she only had to listen for a few minutes before the Valium kicked in. She got the Valium from her friend Nancy Warren, who is not afraid of flying but still has plenty else to worry about.

"There's no way of knowing when something terrible's going to happen," Richard had told Ann. "So you might as well get out there and enjoy." This was his way of trying to reassure her.

"Well, your father said I might as well enjoy myself because I could step off the curb and get hit by a bus anyway," Ann says now, and wonders why she phrased it this way. Something passes across Julie's face that could be annoyance and could be concern. Her eyes have a glassy, slightly drunk look.

"But at least it wouldn't be just any bus," Julie says, and Ann is relieved to see her smile. "It'd be a double-decker."

"Oh, I can't believe it!" Ann cries, as one rolls by their window. "I can't believe we're really here." She's aware that she has said this many, many times since they arrived this morning. On the train from Gatwick, they'd passed through miles of snow-covered meadows and she wanted, crazily, to jump off the train and roll around in the snow. It seemed different than Pennsylvania snow, kinder and more mysterious.

Outside, the flakes have stopped and the sun is seeping around the edge of the clouds, damp and yolky. Julie is almost finished with her cider and Ann wonders if she's going to order another one. How does she drink them so fast?

"Come on," Julie says, "let's go get hit by some buses."

"Oh, don't say that," says Ann, and thinks suddenly of Debra Warren—Nancy and Henry's daughter, Julie's friend—who was hit by a car, a drunk driver who swerved into her Toyota three days before Christmas. She broke her back in two places but she'll live, and she'll walk, but there was a little while when nobody knew for sure. Nancy told Ann that when something like that happens, it makes everything up to that point seem like a streak of good luck.

%

The tube station at Charing Cross is so crowded that Julie loses her mother, trapped between two backpacking teenagers, and doesn't locate her again until they are at the top of the escalator, breathing in the shocking cold air.

"What a crowd!" Julie's mother cries. She looks garishly, ridiculously American: white Nikes, puffy beige coat, red earmuffs and matching mittens, which she is now struggling to put on, holding her purse (also puffy and beige) between her knees. Julie has taken care to dress in a way that she assumed Europeans would dress—all black. Even her black shoes, which aren't nearly as warm as her brown boots with the silly, furry cuffs. Her feet are throbbing mildly, but she feels conspicuously inconspicuous, worldly and disguised.

When they are outside the station, her mother gasps and clutches Julie's arm in a way that seems highly dramatic. Across the street, Trafalgar Square is people- and pigeon-filled; in front of Nelson's Column is the Christmas tree Henry had told her about, huge and skinny and sparkling with tiny white lights. She imagines telling him, "When I saw that tree, I felt my heart drop." Which isn't exactly true, but she does feel excited, and happy, and when she is across the street and can see Big Ben in the distance she closes her eyes, as if she can send him a mental postcard. *I'm here*, she thinks, *and you are not.*

New Year's Eve is the day after tomorrow, and there are barriers set up around the fountains, thick ugly slabs of concrete. "People were always drowning in the fountains," Henry had told her. "They'd jump in and be too drunk to get out."

"Are you afraid that'll happen to me?" she asked him. "If we go?" She was joking but he looked at her sternly and said, "I hope you're smarter than that." Which made her think that after being lovers for seven months they didn't, in many ways, know each other at all. They knew each other's bodies and they knew each other's schedules and the chronology of each other's lives. She had hoped that London would somehow shake loose all the other, mysterious kinds of knowledge, things she couldn't even explain if he asked her to.

She takes a picture of the tree, and the barrier-ed fountains, and her mother standing in front of one of the lions around Nelson's Column. Behind her, a family of Indian children are trying to climb on its back; the mother's robes swirl under her black coat as she hoists the last child up, triumphant. Julie takes a picture of this, too. She turns around and takes a picture of the National Gallery, and the thought of all those paintings Henry loves so much, right there across the street from her, makes her want to cry.

"Quick, look!" her mother shouts, and when Julie looks her mother is shaking with laughter; a pigeon has alighted on her head. Julie snaps another picture and imagines showing Henry, saying, "That could've been *you* with a pigeon on your head." But she can't imagine what he would say back.

"You know," Julie says to her mother, when they are walking down Whitehall, toward the spires of Parliament (next on Henry's list, which Julie carries folded in her pocket), "apparently Trafalgar Square is a big place to go on New Year's Eve. I think it'd be fun."

"Well, sure," says her mother. "Might as well live dangerously." She doesn't sound wholly convinced, but this doesn't matter. Julie has already decided she will go alone if she has to.

%

When Julie was a baby, she used to smash her head against the side of her crib and scream and scream, until Ann picked her up and held her. "Why is she doing that?" she said to Richard. "I'm afraid she's going to hurt herself!"

Richard said it was birth trauma, the effect of being trapped, briefly, in the birth canal.

"She's not going to hold a grudge, is she?" Ann said, mostly kidding, and Richard said, "She might." Then he added, "We'll have something to blame teenage rebellion on."

Ann envisioned a future of police drug raids and phone calls from jail, all her fault. But Julie got over her head bashing within a few months and eventually became a tall, quiet teenager who exhibited no signs of birth canal trauma. (Later, Ann would wonder if Richard had made this up entirely.) And yet sometimes, when she hugged Julie, Ann could feel her daughter shrinking away, her entire body withdrawing from Ann's touch as if it hurt her. Finally she would not allow herself to be touched at all. Richard said this was normal. Richard seemed to think that as long as things were normal, it didn't matter how unhappy you were.

Sometimes Ann wonders what it's like to be one of his patients. She actually considered hiring a woman to go see him and say, "My husband's a workaholic, my daughter won't let me near her, I'm unhappy and I feel helpless!" and see what he told her. She thought of the woman as the Stunt Double. But this seemed like a desperate act, something a nutcase in a soap opera would do. With her luck, he would fall in love with the Stunt Double.

He did fall in love with a patient once, almost seven years ago. This is not something he ever told her, not something they've ever discussed. She doesn't think he ever actually slept with her, or even kissed her. When he and Ann met each other he was living with somebody—a college girlfriend—and they had three months of tortured, platonic coffees before he decided to end things with the girlfriend and be with Ann. "I have never cheated on anybody in my life," he told her solemnly. "I would never do that." His idea of loyalty was to fall in love with someone else but not touch her—at the time, Ann thought this was noble.

But this woman, Beth. She would call him late at night and he would go into his study and talk softly; sometimes Ann heard him laugh. When he came back to bed he would have a thoughtful, amused look on his face, a look Ann remembered from their tortured coffees. On the days he saw Beth (Wednesdays and Fridays; Ann had looked in his appointment book), he would be strangely quiet when he came home, would retreat into his study and shut the door and not be hungry for dinner.

She pictured Beth as a model-thin giraffe of a girl, mid-twenties, trying to recover from an eating disorder and a broken heart. She imagined Richard saying to her, the way he once said to Ann, "I think I must be in love with you, but I don't know what to do about it, and I don't know if you feel the same way."

And Beth saying, as Ann did (staring helplessly into Richard's earnest brown eyes), "I just want to be with you."

But then the calls stopped. Beth's name was gone from his appointment book. Richard returned, gradually, to their dinner table. He even noticed Ann's sadness and suggested she go back to teaching, something she'd loved and hadn't done for thirteen years, since Julie was born. I don't miss teaching, I miss *you*, she thought, but she went back to work anyway. And that's where she met Nancy—tiny and loud-laughed and gorgeously silver-haired, even though she was Ann's age. Nancy taught in the same pod of fourth graders, and she had a daughter a year older than Julie—but so different, so outgoing! It was Debra whom Julie first double-dated with, Debra she used to spend hours at the mall with, and giggle in her room with, listening to rock albums. It was Debra, Ann once thought meanly, who made Julie a normal teenager in the first place.

Henry, Nancy's art-professor husband, reminded Ann of a bird, a crow or a hawk, something dark and swooping. He told long, rambling jokes and cooked an amazing chicken marsala, and he looked at Nancy as if she hung the moon. That's how Richard phrased it, almost wistfully, Ann thought, and she wondered if he was thinking of Beth.

And then something happened. It was as if Nancy and Henry had cast some kind of spell on her and Richard, summoning from them their best qualities. Ann was aware of herself as a funny, interesting woman, a sexy woman. She and Nancy shopped together and both bought the kind of short, breezy dresses Ann thought only teenagers could wear, but which—she had to admit, with a small gasp there in the dressing room at Wards—made her look leggy and beautiful.

And Richard, normally so quiet with company around, was suddenly galvanized, charming and outgoing. He and Henry talked excitedly about books they'd read, books about psychology, art, and astronomy. Sometimes they would all troop down to the backyard and Richard would point out constellations none of them could ever really see. Or else they would go to the Warrens' and swim in their pool. Ann would float on her back and watch the stars twirl overhead and listen to the far-off sounds of their daughters inside, playing rock albums and making (Ann imagined) prank phone calls to boys, and she would think she had never been so effortlessly happy.

Over the years, the two families withdrew more into their own lives, seeing each other at Christmas parties, and at the girls' graduations. Sometimes they'd get together for a swim at the Warrens' house, and last summer they'd had a few dinners together. She and Nancy still meet for coffee nearly every Saturday and go to the occasional happy hour—though Nancy likes drinking more than Ann does. Ann does not like to drink much at all. "Richard thinks it's all about not wanting to be out of control," she told Nancy. "But I think it has more to do with not wanting to puke."

It has occurred to Ann that Nancy knows more about her life than anyone else does. She's even told her about Beth, and Nancy said, "Oh, it's so obvious Richard loves you," which is exactly what Ann wanted to hear, even if she didn't necessarily believe it. And Nancy told her all about her sad teenaged past—abortion, halfhearted suicide attempt, alcoholic father—and meeting Henry her senior year at Ohio State.

Ann feels both protective and intimidated around Nancy, a strange feeling that is almost (this thought comes to her suddenly, walking over the shiny wooden floors of the National Gallery, hearing her daughter's shoes clomping quietly beside her) the way she feels about Julie. And even though there's nothing she could do, even though Debra will be all right, Ann feels slightly guilty, here in London while Nancy is at home.

"Well, you *must* go," Nancy had said. "There's not even a question. You're just looking for an excuse not to have to get on a plane." Henry had cancelled his research trip to Europe, so at least Nancy wouldn't be all alone. "You must go," Nancy said again, firmly, and Ann said oh-what-the-hell.

"My feet hurt," Julie says, slowing down by a painting of a blindfolded woman with flowing red hair. A man is standing by with an axe, ready to cut her head off. "It's too hot in here and my feet *hurt*." She pouts. She sighs loudly, like a small child, and Ann wants to grab her by the coat and pull her close.

Instead she says, "Well then, let's sit down for while."

"You sit down," Julie says nastily. "I'm getting the hell out of here." Then she turns around and clomps back out of the room, toward the Monets and the exit.

Following, Ann tells herself it's not *her* Julie's mad at. It's that other person, the one who was supposed to be here instead.

Julie had been planning this trip since Thanksgiving, with one of her school friends—someone she spoke of vaguely, which made Ann suspect it was a young man. But she didn't know for sure until Julie informed her, crying, that the trip was off, cancelled, her friend couldn't go, didn't want to go, had better things to do. And then Ann said, "It's not such a big deal—look at what happened to Debra!" which made Julie cry harder.

"I'll go to London with you," Ann had said, shocked at herself, and equally amazed when Julie said, through ragged sobs, "Will you? Will you really? Oh, thank you!"

When she'd told Julie in the pub that she was trying to make it seem real, she didn't mean so much the place—though certainly that, too—but the fact of Julie wanting her here.

That first night, she awakens when it's still dark outside, her body confused by the time change. She gets out of bed and goes to the window and draws back the thick, pink draperies. The sky behind the glass is faintly red; in the house across the street—another bed and breakfast?—someone is watching television. Ann thinks how strange it is to be awake in the middle of the night, in a country where the only person who knows you is sleeping—how you can feel less lonely than you would expect, less lonely even than you're used to.

%

They go to the places on Henry's list. The Tower of London, St. Paul's Cathedral, Madame Tussaud's. Julie buys postcards to give Henry when she's back; she writes things like *England is glorious but freezing!* and *I stood on Tower Bridge and thought of you.* She doesn't put his name or address on them. She signs them all "Love." When her mother asks whom she's writing to (they are in a pub again, this time in ritzy Hampstead, another of Henry's haunts), Julie says, "Just some people from school."

She's aware of her mother wanting something from her—information, but something else, too—and the thrill of withholding it. Julie experiences moments when she forgets that she had wanted her mother to come with her; she wants to say *Leave me alone, go home.* It's that same feeling she used to get when they were shopping for school clothes together, or when her parents came to her college for homecoming week and Julie had to show them around, wishing the whole time that they would just leave.

Then there is that other part of her that wishes her mother would get drunk with her and tell her things. Personal things. About what it's like to be married to Julie's father, about her love life before that. Did she ever think of leaving him? Did she ever have an affair? Did he?

At the Hampstead pub Julie excuses herself to buy cigarettes from the machine. She has never smoked in front of her mother and expects (hopes?) to be met with dismay and disapproval. But all her mother says is, "I didn't know you smoked. Seems like everybody in this country does, huh?"

There have been occasions—though rare—when her mother has surprised her in this way. When she'd announced she would come to London, for instance. "If you're sure you still want to go," her mother had said. And Julie, who couldn't stand the thought of staying home, who had imagined the trip so thoroughly that she could almost believe she didn't need Henry there at all, said she was sure. And what also surprised Julie was how grateful she felt, and how she had almost (or at least she'd thought about it) confessed everything. Not that she would, or could, or even wants to now.

In Camden Town she sees someone who looks like him and she says, boldly, "Doesn't that man look like Henry Warren?" She feels her heart stall when she says his name. She wants to say it again.

"Oh, it does," says Julie's mother.

It does. And after that Julie sees him everywhere. Or younger versions of him—wearing scarves, and smoking. He'd once shown her a picture of himself when he was twenty, her age. In the picture he has long, Beatle-ish sideburns and a goatee; he looks mildly amused, and Julie wondered if a woman had taken the picture, someone beautiful, wearing go-go boots. This is what she pictures of his London days. She thinks (though he didn't tell her this) of him drifting through the carnival of sixties' London all spaced out on acid, with some black-haired, racoon-eyed girl striding fast beside him, clutching his hand. She finds this image overwhelmingly romantic.

What would have happened if they had been twenty at the same time? "We would have hated each other," he'd said. "Or rather, you would have hated me. I wouldn't have appreciated you."

He made himself sound dangerous and womanizing, but he was married by the time he was twenty-two and Debra was born when he was twenty-four. And when he told Julie she was the only woman he's ever cheated on Nancy with, she believed him.

"You kissed me first," he reminded her once, when things were just beginning.

"You didn't have to take it personally," she said. "I was so drunk I'd've kissed anybody."

She had meant this as a joke, but that's not the way it sounded, and perhaps she had actually wanted to hurt him a little. She was feeling both powerful and helpless, a feeling that hasn't diminished at all in the months they've been together.

She did kiss him first, and this still amazes her when she thinks of it. And it was only last June, though it seems like years ago, like something that happened when she was a different person. Henry had come over for dinner, bringing Caesar salad and white wine, and the four of them—Henry, Julie, her mother and father—had eaten barbequed chicken at the table on the front porch. The sun went down and instead of turning on the porch light, Julie's mother brought out two candles, one white and one purple, which Julie recognized from last Christmas's Advent wreath. It was the first time Henry had come over alone—Nancy was visiting some relative in Ohio, Debra was living up at school for the summer—and he seemed shyer than Julie had ever seen him. He giggled nervously and kept dropping his napkin, and when he looked at Julie, his eyes glinting orange in the flickering candlelight, she felt as if a fist had reached inside her chest and squeezed her heart. That's how she described it to him later; that's the only way she could describe it.

She hasn't confessed that she's loved him since the seventh grade, something she finds both shameful and prophetic. This is a secret she was saving to tell him, something she would say when they were standing on Tower Bridge together, in the fog. "That first time you came over to pick up Debra, and I opened the door and saw you—" But she isn't sure what to say next. "I knew I loved you" sounds too hokey. "I wanted you" isn't right either, and not even accurate. What she felt the first time she saw Henry at the door was almost fear—or it seemed like fear. She had never seen anyone so tall, so smiley and rumpled. His black hair was half in his eyes, and his face was stubbly. It didn't dawn on her until later that he reminded her of a magician she'd seen on TV, who'd made an elephant vanish.

But she would never tell him that the first time she'd seen him she'd been afraid and that she'd run to her room after he and Debra had left and lay on her bed, feeling dizzy. Or that sometimes when she and Debra were swimming in the Warrens' pool, she'd float on her back with her eyes closed, imagining him watching her. She had assumed that the right words would come to her, at the right time. Maybe just "I've loved you longer than you know." Or maybe now she won't have the chance to tell him at all, a thought she finds oddly relieving.

The first time she'd kissed him, that night only last June, she had been very, very drunk. She drank almost his entire bottle of wine by herself and was feeling warm and funny and fun, and when she saw that Henry's wallet had fallen out of his pocket, she calmly scooted it with her foot right off the porch into the snapdragons. She helped her parents carry the plates inside, and they all waved good-bye to Henry, who drove off tooting his horn twice, his headlights sweeping over the lawn. Her parents went inside, telling her to blow out the candles before she went to bed. Julie retrieved Henry's wallet from the snapdragons. She didn't know why she had hidden it. She just wanted it, but now that she had it she couldn't bring herself to look through it, at the inevitable pictures of Nancy and Debra. And then his headlights were beaming up the driveway, and he was back, asking, "Did I drop my wallet around here?"

He told her later that she looked beautiful, standing there on the lawn in her sundress. (She wasn't wearing a sundress, she was wearing shorts, but she's pleased that he remembers her this way.) He said her hair was glowing, the moon was so bright. He sat on the porch steps with her and sighed heavily, happily, and Julie threw her head back and looked at the sky. Every star had a double floating beside it; two moons hung between the trees at the edge of the yard.

They must have talked for a while, because Julie can recall the sort of silence that comes after something has been revealed, a silence both urgent and calm. And then she was kissing him, thinking that the air smelled like Christmas. The candles had burned themselves out. She hadn't expected herself to do this, or for him to kiss back; she hadn't expected to feel so devastated when he stood up suddenly and made his way across the slope of her front yard, back to his car. And she had certainly not expected him to call her the next day and ask if she wanted to have coffee somewhere.

But after that they had the sort of affair she did expect—quick nights in motel rooms, long phone conversations when she went back to school in the fall. He drove out there on occasional weekends and they stayed at a motel and made love on the stiff, tan bedspread. She did not think of him as Debra's father, or Mr. Warren, or the husband of her mother's friend. It was as if he were someone entirely new, someone she had only just met, or invented. She never told him about kicking his wallet off the porch, and she understands that she never will.

She was glad her friendship with Debra had ended a couple of years ago. Or, rather, they maintained a sort of friendship that existed out of tradition; when they saw each other they talked mostly about the past, remember this and remember that. Secretly, Julie thought Debra was boring and not very smart, studying occupational therapy at some private college near Lancaster. Julie visited her once, during her first semester, and all there was to do (or all Debra knew about; Julie suspected that she was not exactly clued in to the party possibilities) was sit around in her dorm room and drink root beer schnapps with Debra's roommate, a pudgy girl with dorky teddy bears displayed on her bed. Debra was wearing a black Bon Jovi T-shirt; she kept sprinting down to the snack machine on the second floor for red licorice. Julie did four shots of root beer schnapps and then feigned being asleep on the floor until she actually was.

It was the mothers who stayed fast friends, shopping together and talking on the phone, an adult version of the friendship she and Debra had seemed headed for, once. When she sees Nancy, Julie sometimes formulates the words in her head: *I am sleeping with your husband*, as a dare to herself, an experiment. Or the reverse: *You are married to a man who loves me*. But it never seems quite real, as if there are two separate Henrys, hers and Nancy's, each with no knowledge of the other one.

Today, when her mother announces she's going to call Nancy from an authentic British phone booth, Julie has the first real pang of terrible, aching jealousy. She wishes again that her mother was not here, was not talking to Nancy Warren (Is Henry in the room? Can he hear the conversation?), that she was here by herself. Why had she wanted her mother to come at all? Was she so afraid of being alone? That was it, of course: the fear not just of being alone but being lonely. She supposes she wanted some sort of comfort as well, some reassurance that everything would work out for the best. But this is a ridiculous thing to expect, and now she feels as if she's made a terrible mistake. If her mother wasn't here, she could go from pub to pub, making friends. She could return home changed, braver. If her mother wasn't here, Julie thinks, she would be having adventures, and would not be thinking about Henry Warren at all.

Julie buys postcards while her mother talks, scenes of St. Paul's Cathedral at sunset and punks with green hair. When her mother finds her, she says, "Debra's going to be fine, it looks like." Then: "Tried your father but he wasn't home." She looks suddenly sad, standing there in her saggy coat, flipping absently through the postcard selection. Julie feels a baffling wave of tenderness, and she wonders where it came from, and if it's meant for someone else.

⁂

On the television in their room they watch the news—twelve people frozen to death in Europe, another woman (also from Kent, like that doomed, dog-loving couple) found dead in her car, stranded on a remote, snow-covered road. Ann says, "Such a shame," and looks over at Julie, who is lying on her bed reading a tabloid with pictures of cavorting royalty.

Ann tells herself it's ridiculous to be disappointed—what had she expected, anyway? They've seen the crown jewels, and the changing of the guard! Things she thought she'd never see. And it's not as if Julie's ignoring her, or mad at her. Though this afternoon she'd had the brief, painful thought that she was trying to lose her, to get away; but she was only looking for postcards.

At a phone booth near Highgate Cemetery (one of the rare red booths; they all seemed to be made of glass) Ann had phoned Richard, who wasn't home, and then Nancy, who was.

"We're going to Trafalgar Square tomorrow night," she shouted, even though the connection was fine.

Nancy said Debra was doing great, would probably be home in a week or two.

"Well thank God," Ann breathed, and it seemed as if everything was suddenly perfect again, as perfect as things could be. And then she said, "We should all come here, together."

"To England?" said Nancy.

"To Europe! Wouldn't that be great? Maybe when Julie graduates?" And it suddenly seemed not only possible but as if it had already been decided—the six of them, Debra too, traveling through Europe together the summer after next. "Paris!" Ann cried, and Nancy laughed on the other end and said that would be fun.

"Did I tell you," Ann tells Julie now, though she thinks she's already mentioned it, "that we might do Europe with the Warrens next summer?"

"*Do* Europe?" Julie says. "What does that mean?" And then she rises from her bed and announces, "I'm going out for a while."

Ann does not say *Be careful* or *Take money for the phone* or *Don't forget your map.* She does not ask how late she'll be or where she's going. She says, "Good-bye," and when Julie leaves she turns off the television and reads about the cavorting royalty, and then tries to sleep.

%

Two weeks ago (though it seems like so much longer), when they were planning this trip, Henry told Julie the story of Elizabeth Siddal, the model and wife of Dante Gabriel Rossetti.

"Every man needs a model wife," Julie said, and then wished she hadn't. But Henry wasn't paying attention, he was flipping through a book of paintings (they were in his office; the Fine Arts Building was closed and quiet for the break) of a heavy-lidded, tragic-looking woman with auburn hair so thick and beautiful it looked like something alive.

"He loved her so much," Henry said, "that when she died he buried his love poems with her. He put them next to her cheek."

He looked at her then, and Julie almost expected him to reach out and touch *her* cheek; but Henry is not prone to predictable affection, and this is one of the things Julie has found to love about him. She always feels as if something is happening that is just beyond her comprehension, some undercurrent of feeling that can't be interpreted in any obvious gesture.

What did it mean, him telling her this story?

At the time, she thought he was saying something about the sacrifices love costs you, and how you make them willingly.

This afternoon, walking through the tangled, gothic graves at Highgate Cemetery with her mother, Julie heard the tour guide tell the rest of the story. How, seven years after Elizabeth's death, Rossetti decided he wanted the poems back, and had her exhumed.

"That's something," said Julie's mother. They walked on in the harsh winter sunlight, Julie's feet suddenly freezing in their black, English-looking shoes.

Had he forgotten to tell her that part? Did he even know? Of course he must know; he was writing a book about them. He knew and he didn't tell her because it wasn't romantic; because the truth,

Julie thinks bitterly, is that whatever you give up for love you eventually want back.

She thinks this now, in the throng of the Leicester Square tube station, and she allows herself to be swept into a current of bundled, laughing people, past the brasseries of Long Acre right into Covent Garden. When Henry told her about Covent Garden, she'd pictured a green, flowered place—an actual garden, with fountains and statues. She hadn't imagined cobblestones or jugglers, or green-haired dogs, or loud pubs, or busloads of tourists. If Henry were here they would be having a drink now, perhaps in one of these pubs. But then she thinks they wouldn't, because she would have figured it out—that he doesn't really love her, that he wants his life back the way it was. And she would have gone out alone, and she would be right here.

This thought cheers her. She goes into a pub and stands at the bar, which is the only available place to stand, and smokes three cigarettes and drinks two pints of cider. And she feels that she is adventurous, and she feels lonely. No one talks to her. Two pale, dark-haired boys in leather jackets seem to be looking at her but then they're gone. She leaves and wanders all the way to Piccadilly, stopping at another pub for another cider, which she drinks fast because she's aware that she is the only person who is alone, here or (it seems) anywhere.

"Some people are better off alone," she'd said to Henry once, speaking of her parents. She had never said that to anyone before, that sometimes she wishes her parents would divorce. "For their own sake," she said. This seemed to her very astute, and she wanted Henry to think her wise and insightful. But all he'd said was, "I think people figure out what they need to be happy. Eventually," he added. And she'd felt again that he was telling her something important, about the two of them.

Julie does not dislike her parents. Her father is a kind, vague figure, mostly absent; her mother is prone to annoying clingy-ness. She imagines that if they divorced, her father would live happily alone someplace, in a bachelor pad with a small dog (he loves dogs, her mother's allergic). Her mother would get out and make more friends—someone besides Nancy Warren, who Julie has never really liked; she's always smiling out of one side of her mouth in a wise-cracking way. Julie suspects Nancy has grown tired of her mother's eager friendship, though she has no proof of this.

"Sometimes," Julie said to Henry, "really great people just do not belong together." Then she wondered if he thought she meant him and Nancy, if she was hinting that *they* should get divorced. Which she wasn't, or at least she didn't think so. She didn't want to marry Henry Warren, but she couldn't say what exactly she did want.

Julie is drunk. She smokes on the way to the tube station and when she gets there it's closed, a metal grate blocking the entrance. And then all there is to do is walk, though she has no idea where she is, or where her bed and breakfast is from here. The thought comes to her that she could call Henry and tell him where she is (just outside the Trocadero, a shiny shopping arcade that reminds her of the glitziest malls back home) and let him tell her which bus to take back. She has never called him, not once. That's one of the things that has been agreed upon without being mentioned.

If she calls him he'll tell her (she knows this, can hear his voice in her head), "Just ask someone which bus to take!" He'll be annoyed that she called, at whatever hour of the day or night it is there.

She won't call him, but she won't follow his imagined advice, either. People are flowing down the sidewalk, beautiful English men with scarves swirled around their necks. There's a bus stop across the street and she goes to it, then gets on the first bus that stops and climbs—shakily—the winding steps to the top.

It takes an hour and a half and two more buses before she is able to find her way back to Belsize Park, and when she gets off she is almost sober. She walks back thinking that she needs to be kissed by one of those beautiful English men, and hoping her mother has not been awake all this time worrying. Thinking also that they do not have to see any more of the things on that list—which she has already, without even meaning to, lost.

Ann is startled out of a light sleep by the ringing phone: Richard, saying he'd just gotten her message, he's sorry he missed her call, what time is it there?

"I don't know," she says, fumbling in the dark for her glowing alarm clock, not finding it. "I was sleeping."

"Oh, sorry—crap. It's five hours *later* there, I forgot. Are you having fun? How's Julie?"

"Julie's out. She went out exploring."

Then she feels a stab of worry; she has located her clock. It's ten-forty-five and the tube trains stop running at eleven. The thought comes to her that if anything has happened to Julie it will be her fault—because she did not tell her to take maps, or change, or to be careful. She says to Richard, "I was tired so she went alone."

"What's there to do in London at this hour?" Richard says lightly, as if he doesn't quite believe her.

"Oh, this is a hopping place," Ann tells him. "Open all night, so I hear."

Richard says there's nothing exciting to report, the house seems too quiet, he misses her. When Ann asks if he's been to the hospital to see Debra, he says yes and she knows he's lying. His lying voice is something that has recently become obvious to her, though he uses it (so far) for rather small, ridiculous things. Yes, he's sure he bought stamps; no, he didn't hear the phone; yes, he's been to the hospital.

"You didn't ask about the flight," Ann remembers suddenly. "You didn't ask how I managed to fly across the ocean without losing it."

"Well!" Richard says cheerfully. "I was just getting around to that." (A lie.) "How was the flight?"

"Piece of cake," Ann says.

When they hang up it's impossible to go back to sleep, not with the clock flickering past eleven, and eleven-thirty. When Julie was little, Ann used to lie awake thinking of all the terrible things that could befall her, as if the very thought of them could, like a magic charm, prevent them from happening. Drowning, kidnapping, electrocution, fire. Then, when Julie was older, the list changed: drunk driving, rape, plane crashes, car crashes. After Debra's accident, Nancy had said, "You never expect this to happen," and Ann had thought—irrationally—*But that's why it did.*

Now, she lies wide awake and realizes there will never be an end to the list, that she will always be able to conjure some horrible accident, some shadowy stranger dragging Julie away, something falling from the sky. She tries, now, to imagine Julie safe. She pictures her on a bus, looking out the window at the lights of London, smiling. She is still awake at twelve-fifteen when Julie comes in the door; she hears shoes plop on the floor. The light snaps on, then off; then Julie shuts the door and makes her way down the hall to the bathroom.

Ann does not hear her come back; she sleeps until late morning and wakes with Julie sitting beside her on the bed, saying hurry, get up, the pubs are almost open.

※

It's New Year's Eve and Julie wants to spend the entire day in pubs. "Until the last possible minute, and then we'll go join the maddened throng."

"Maddened?" says her mother.

"Crazed," Julie says. "Drunken, like us."

Julie's mother does not want to spend the day in pubs; she wants to go to Kensington Gardens or maybe take a boat ride on the canal from Camden Lock. "Or we could go to the zoo," she says. She has a book called *You in London* and it says the zoo is worth seeing.

The zoo was not on Henry's list, so Julie agrees. Then it turns out you can take the boat ride to the zoo, so that's what they end up doing. It seems even colder than the previous days; Julie has abandoned her black shoes for her Nikes; side by side with her mother in the boat, their feet look identical.

"I was thinking," Julie says, when they are wandering around the Penguin Pool, "that we could maybe take a day-trip tomorrow. To Canterbury or someplace. Maybe even stay overnight, and take a bus to the airport."

"I'd love to see Canterbury!"

Julie came up with this idea last night, when she was on the bus (the right one, finally) back to Belsize Park. The idea of leaving the city entirely.

After the zoo it's late afternoon and they're hungry; Julie's mother agrees to start pubbing. Julie picks a place near Charing Cross, so they can make their way toward Trafalgar Square. There's a Christmas tree and a fireplace and an old couple sitting with their dog (a beige terrier with a red bow stuck on its head), and they're smoking and chattering in a language that sometimes sounds like English and sometimes doesn't. Julie and her mother eat cheesy baked potatoes. They drink a pint of sweet cider (Julie) and a glass of white wine (her mother), and then they go to another pub, and another one. And Julie tells her mother about being lost the night before, about riding on the top of a double-decker bus and not knowing where she was.

"I thought about you on a bus!" her mother interrupts suddenly. "It was sort of a dream. You were looking out a bus window and smiling."

"I don't think I was smiling," Julie says. "But maybe I was. Once I figured out where I was going."

She doesn't tell her mother that she was lonely, or that she wished some man in a pub would talk to her. She doesn't say she was afraid her mother had stayed awake, worrying. She feels cocooned in a dopey happiness, and when she goes to the bar for another cider, she gets one for her mother, too.

"It's sweet," she tells her. "Like apple juice."

"I haven't even finished my wine!" her mother says, and giggles. "I hope I don't start dancing on tables."

"I'll dance with you," Julie says, and presents her glass for clinking. "Cheers. Bottoms up."

"Down the hatch!"

"Glug glug," Julie says.

"Oh, I forgot!" Her mother wipes the back of her hand across her mouth, like a child. "Your father called last night, while you were out. He said he saw Debra in the hospital and she's doing real well."

"Do you miss Dad?" Julie asks, and feels an odd thrill when her mother hesitates.

"Of course," she says at last. And then: "Sort of," which makes them both laugh.

Julie has never seen her mother drunk, and suspects she never has been. She feels, in her happy, blurry state, that some connection has occurred between them, artificially induced but genuine nonetheless, something that's been coaxed out of hiding. Outside, the sky is thickening and darkening, and the lights are glowing and taxis are swinging past the window. Julie is about to say something about how it's already New Year's in Australia when her mother leans forward and says earnestly, "This person who was supposed to go on the trip with you."

"Yes?" Julie says, and it suddenly seems like a dream she had once—a familiar dream—but all she knows is what comes next, not how it ends.

"It was somebody you cared about very much, wasn't it?"

Her mother's face is glowing pink; her eyes look watery, as if she's about to sneeze or cry. Julie knows as soon as she starts talking that she will not be able to stop until she's said everything; realizes, too, that this was why she'd wanted to get drunk with her mother in the first place, so she'd be able to tell her, so she wouldn't be able to stop herself from telling.

Her mother says nothing.

Later, Julie will not be able to remember exactly what she said, how she phrased things, how much she revealed. She will hope she didn't mention the motel rooms, or the fact that she kissed him first, or that she kicked his wallet off the porch. But she will never be entirely sure, and it's not something she can ever ask.

%

Big Ben is frozen. This news reaches Ann through a blur of alcohol and earmuffs, and at first she thinks she can't have heard correctly. But it's true—or everyone seems to think so—and a cry of collective dismay carries through the crowd. It's almost two hours until midnight, but the square is already full. (It seems full, but the next day Ann will see photographs and realize just how much fuller it could get.) The air is cold and sour, and Ann wonders if it's her own breath she's smelling. She wonders if she'll be sick the next day; she wonders if she'll ever feel well again.

Julie has gone. Back to the bed and breakfast—or maybe somewhere else, Ann doesn't know. Maybe she's here, in the crowd somewhere, part of the maddened throng—wasn't that how she'd phrased it? Drunken, she'd said. Like us. And now Ann is the drunken one, the maddened one.

When Julie told her about Henry, the first thing Ann could think to say was, "Does Debra know?" Which was, of course, a ridiculous question, but no more ridiculous than the fact that Julie was having an affair with Henry Warren. "Does she?"

"Mother!" said Julie, as if she were the one who was offended, as if Ann had just said something horrible to *her*.

And the thought came to Ann that somehow everything was connected—that the affair was to blame for Debra's car accident, in some awful, mysterious way.

"I am," Ann said slowly, to herself more than Julie, "a complete idiot. A complete and total idiot. I am so dumb. Why am I so dumb?"

"You're not dumb," Julie said. "Don't cry, there's no point crying."

Ann, who had not considered crying, considered it now and was surprised and relieved to realize this was not something she was going to do. She was not sad; she was pissed, she was shocked. She stared at her daughter and wondered what clues she'd been missing for seven months. Wondered if Julie and Henry had ever had sex in their house, or in his, when Nancy was out. (Nancy, who must be told immediately—or never told, Ann doesn't know, can't think.)

"That man looks like Henry Warren," Julie had said, and Ann had not known even then. Henry, going to Europe the same week!

"I am *dumb*," Ann cried. "But you! Christ!"

"I didn't tell you this so you could yell at me," Julie said quietly.

"Why did you tell me? What did you think I would say?" Ann was aware of her voice, loud and desperate as someone calling for help. "You must stop this," she said, quieter now, unable to use the words *affair, love, Henry*. "You must stop. You must."

"Well, I will," Julie said. "I mean, that's what I've decided, that's why I told you about it." (But why tell her now, when she's drunk? Unable to defend herself, to think clearly. If she were sober she might know who to hate, and who to pity, and what to do.) "You're always saying, 'You can tell me anything! I'll love you no matter what!' Was that a crock of shit?"

"I'll love you no matter what," Ann said slowly, "but no—you can't tell me anything."

And that's when Julie got up and left, just left Ann sitting there, drunk, somewhere on Charing Cross Road. She left the pub feeling wobbly, and made her way toward Trafalgar Square—looking for Julie, to tell her she was sorry (was she?) and couldn't they talk about this tomorrow, when she could think again?

Now, so cold the inside of her mouth aches, it seems to Ann that there is something she must do, that Julie told her this so that she could take some sort of action. But what? Tell Nancy? Have a talk with Henry? She feels a wave of rage—toward Henry and Julie and Nancy, who should have known, and Richard, who should have noticed. And mostly herself, because she has done something wrong—failed to plan for this disaster and therefore, somehow, allowed it to happen.

She leaves well before midnight, and it isn't until the next day that she learns Big Ben was, in fact, frozen but that it thawed—a miracle—just before midnight. But on the train back to Belsize Park she isn't thinking about Big Ben; she is thinking that she will never come back to England, never.

And she's right, she never does. She will never travel to Europe again, or even take a plane. (The flight home is uneventful—though she almost hopes the plane goes down, she almost thinks that would be the easiest thing.) And when, years later, Julie gets married in California, Ann takes a train all the way across the country, alone. The trip takes almost a week, and Ann thinks with some amazement that this is the first time she's traveled by herself. She has taken a few short trips with men since her divorce—car trips to New York or Lake Erie or Atlantic City. She has not had to explain that she will not fly; she has never been asked.

On the train she meets a couple going to New Mexico for the hot air balloon show and a mother taking her three daughters to San

Francisco to visit her family. She meets two teenage girls who tell her about their boyfriends, who play in a band and want them to be in the video. She meets a man who tells her he always takes trains, it's the only way to see the country. He grins at her, and she notices that his teeth are faintly stained but perfectly straight. "Maybe I'll see you on the way back east," he says. He's young, too young to be flirting, but she allows herself to consider the possibility that he is. When he gets off in Los Angeles, lugging his giant backpack, he waves one strong, grimy hand at her and wishes her luck.

Ann takes out her book but holds it open on her lap, looking out the window, and she thinks that this is definitely the best way to travel.

Vines

Their house sat on the beach, behind three palm trees, in a shade that came and went with the winds. Ronald flew an airplane and his wife, Haley, who grew tomatoes, could look up and see the shadow of his plane flying over her garden. It wasn't easy growing a tomato garden right on the beach, but she had read a lot of books and taken some gardening classes at the community college, so she knew what she was doing. She used a very rare and special dirt that she made herself, and the winds blew enough that the palm trees provided just the right amount of shade.

Every day, Ronald got in his plane and scoured the seas for anyone who might be drowning, or for ships that were in trouble. It wasn't a job he got paid for—he had enough money from his late father's baked-bean emporium—but it was one he took very seriously. Just last month, a cruise ship full of chefs had sunk, and if Ronald hadn't been flying his plane right then, they all would have drowned. The ocean was strewn with herbs and vegetables and chefs, bobbing frantically and screaming, waving spatulas and corkscrews. Ronald called the Coast Guard on his radio and flew around in circles until they arrived in boats to scoop up the chefs.

When he told his wife what he'd done, she insisted he invite the chefs over for dinner. They used up every last tomato on her vines, for their sauces and soups. They baked bread and made hors d'oeuvres with cheese sauces and tiny fish, and clapped each other on the back and stuck their fingers in the pots while they cooked.

For the occasion, Ronald drove across the beach to the liquor store and bought wine, and Haley pulled out the folding chairs, and they all sat late into the night, talking—some of the chefs could speak English—and enjoying the food, most of which was tomato-based. Later, inside the house, Haley and Ronald made love, while the chefs slept on the beach, rolled in blankets. The next morning the chefs got in their van and drove away, tooting their horn, leaving behind their dirty pots and pans, and a garden full of empty vines.

Haley and Ronald met four years ago, in a dating class. Ronald was there because even though he was rich, he wasn't very attractive—he was ugly—and women dumped him after he'd bought them presents. They told him he didn't have enough personality to make up for his ugliness, so he was hoping this class would help him have more personality, at least on dates. At least on a first date.

Haley was there because even though she was very beautiful, she had a terrible, terrible secret: for three days every year, everything she touched turned to dirt. This had, of course, created problems in all of her relationships; as a child she had ruined her mother's necklaces, her father's shoes, her sister's prom dress. She'd been trying it on, six years old, and it turned to dirt right on her, crumbling away and leaving her standing naked in front of the mirror. Her sister had threatened to throw her out the window, then screamed nonstop until their mother took her to J. C. Penny for another, even more expensive, dress. It was kept locked in the armoire, along with the other things Haley was not allowed to touch. The one thing that didn't turn to dirt at her touch was human flesh. But only *human* flesh; she'd reduced five cats and two dogs to mulch by the time she was two.

For three days every year, Haley's mother and father kept her home from school, put her in a tent in the backyard where she couldn't do any damage. In the winter, they set up a heater for her. In the summer, she was instructed to play in the dirt that was already there, and when she was finished they used it on their garden.

There was, unfortunately, never any way of predicting when the three dirt-days would happen.

When she was sixteen, she let a neighbor boy take her to McDonald's and was just getting over her nervousness when her Big Mac crumbled into soil. The boy tried to ignore it—he was very polite—but she was afraid to touch his car so she walked home, and he thought that was rude.

She hadn't been on a date since, and she was twenty-five years old. She hoped to learn some skills in this class about how to meet men she could communicate with, men who would accept her for who she was and not think her rude when she refused to touch their cars.

In the first class, the instructor paired up the students and made them interview each other. She ended up with the ugliest man she'd ever seen, who told her he wanted to meet a woman who saw him for who he was on the inside; she told him about her Terrible Secret, and he took hold of her hands and kissed them. They didn't go to any of the other classes. They got married and moved to the beach, and Ronald bought an airplane with his late father's fortune, and Haley grew tomatoes, and for a while everything was perfect.

Two months after the chefs left, Haley realized she was pregnant. When she told her husband, they cried for happiness and for despair, because what if their baby had to suffer as they'd suffered? What if she turned her crib to dirt, what if no one liked her, what if she grew up ugly and afraid? Then they vowed that they would never keep her outside in a tent, and they would tell her she was beautiful even if she was not, even if it meant hiding mirrors from her.

But then the baby was born, a girl, and she *was* beautiful. They named her Stacy. A year passed, and she grew hair and teeth and learned how to say words, and nothing turned to dirt in her grasp. And, better still, nothing turned to dirt in Haley's grasp, either. She thought maybe, somehow, she might have missed those three days, but the next year again nothing happened, and then the next, until she realized she was cured.

Stacy loved tomatoes; she'd crawl around outside in the summer and eat them off the vine. And when she was older, Haley told her the story of the chefs who came to their house the night she was conceived, and how they made tomato soup and tomato sauce and tomato-and-cheese dips, and fish with tomatoes. Stacy wanted to hear that story over and over. She listened rapt, her face and mouth covered with seeds and juice, her eyes as wild as the bobbing, soupy sea.

%

As the years went by, Ronald continued to fly his plane, and the beach became more and more crowded with tourists, some of whom came from far away to buy Haley's sauces. Stacy went to school, and when she was eighteen she told her parents she wanted to move to Paris and become a chef.

Ronald and Haley were not happy. "Can't you go to the community college?" Haley asked her, knowing she was asking the impossible. Because Stacy needed to know more than Haley or the noncredit cooking classes could teach her; she needed to use spices Haley had never heard of, oils from exotic lands, leaves from trees that grew far away. She needed to learn about puddings and cakes, things that went beyond tomatoes, things tomatoes had no use for.

So she went. Her parents stood on the beach and watched the sliver of her jumbo jet vanish over the water, and five days later they got a postcard of the Eiffel Tower.

Condos were going up all over the beach, and sometimes camera crews filmed TV shows there. Haley and Ronald were asked to sell their house, and they said no, so a construction crew cut down their palm trees instead and built a Sno-Cone stand and parking lot. Next to that was a kiosk where you could get your picture made into a key chain.

When Stacy left, the tomatoes didn't grow as well, and when the palm trees came down they didn't grow at all. Haley bought Miracle-

Gro, but that didn't work. And even though they were rich, they felt starved, and even though they were together, they felt alone. Stacy called rarely, and her voice was sounding different, foreign and staticky and annoyed. She told her parents she couldn't see them anymore because they made her feel strange and unwell, and why couldn't they be like other parents? Why couldn't they go out to movies with friends? Why didn't they move to New York or someplace exciting?

Sometimes she sent them canned tomatoes, but they weren't the same, and they weren't enough.

%

There was something wrong with Haley. She felt old and tired and sad. Ronald asked, "What can I get you?" but she couldn't think of anything she wanted except her daughter and tomatoes, and since Stacy would not come home, Ronald flew over the countryside looking for the best tomatoes he could find. He'd bring them to her in her bed, on a golden plate. She'd take one weary bite and then shake her head and fall back against her pillows. But Ronald had noticed something: when he flew his plane across their garden, the tomatoes grew a little. He told this to Haley, and she struggled out of bed with a look on her face that made him want to weep.

"Would you?" she asked, and he would.

He flew and he flew, and because he loved her so much, cruise ships sank and children floated out to sea in their blow-up rafts. And finally Haley couldn't remember his face at all, and it was as if all she'd ever loved was the angel-shaped shadow that cast itself across her garden, and made it grow.

Midnight, Licorice, Shadow

"Midnight, Licorice, Shadow," she says. "Cocoa, Casper, Dr. Livingston."

"Alfred Hitchcock," he says. "Dracula. Vincent Price."

They have had the cat for nearly three days.

"Cinderblock?" she tries. "Ice bucket?"

It's useless. The harder they try to think of a name, the more elusive it becomes.

"Tomorrow, then," Jeremy says. "If we don't have a name by tomorrow morning, it's bye-bye, Mr. Kitty. No offense, Cupcake," he tells the cat, and gives it a quick rub on the head.

Donna looks at the animal, sprawled on the orange motel carpet like a black bearskin rug. One of his fangs is showing. His monkey paws are kneading at the air.

"Monkey Paw!" she says, but Jeremy is already headed out the door, car keys jangling. He'd invited her to go along—there's some house in Redlands he wants to check out—but she wants to stay with the cat, who now has his eyes closed in feline ecstasy and is purring louder than the air conditioner. She doesn't want to leave him (Merlin? Jasper?) all alone in a strange motel. In an hour or so she'll walk across the parking lot to the Carrows and get a chef's salad for her and a cheeseburger for Jeremy (he always comes back hungry) and maybe she'll give some of her dinner to the cat. They've been feeding him dry food because, as Jeremy says, wet food makes a cat's shits stinkier. Donna thinks the cat's shits are stinky enough as it is.

Still, she likes him. She wants the three of them to drive off together tomorrow morning, like a family on vacation. So far, they've traveled over five hundred miles together, the cat curled up on Donna's lap while Jeremy drives.

If she can just come up with his name, the way she came up with her own. She was born Lacey Love and changed her name to Donna when she left home at sixteen. She liked the wholesome, 1950s' sound of it, the name of a girl in a song. Sometimes she thinks about changing it again, to something more serious: Joan, perhaps, or Agnes. More and more, she feels like a Joan or an Agnes.

"Tango," she says to the cat. "Flower. Bambi. Mr. Jarvis."

The cat jerks his head up and fixes his yellow eyes on hers in what seems like an accusatory way, but she tells herself he must have heard something outside that startled him, something too faint for human ears.

When they first met, she had almost told Jeremy that her name was Sunshine—partly as a joke but partly because she *felt* like a Sunshine right then, surrounded by wildflowers by the side of I-10, halfway between Tucson and Phoenix.

"I would have believed you," he told her later. "Because you are my sunshine. My *only* sunshine," he added, in a low growl. He was prone to saying cheesy things, but he said them in a way that seemed mean and dangerous, and therefore struck her as truthful. For instance, the first time he called her his soul mate, he had his right hand around her neck, and he squeezed just enough to let her know he meant business. "I *know* things about you," he said to her, staring her in the eyes, and she knew those things had nothing to do with any part of her past—certainly not the Lacey Love part of her past—but with who she was at that moment, Donna with Jeremy's hand on her neck.

The things Jeremy knows about her are more mysterious and important than the things he doesn't know. He doesn't know, for instance, that she'd been married and divorced at eighteen, though she would certainly have told him if he asked. He's never asked about her family or her childhood, which she finds refreshing. Why did men always pretend they cared about that? If they could get you to spill one childhood memory, they figured they could get you into bed.

And she always lied about the childhood memory anyway, making something up about her dog being smashed by her father's Oldsmobile when she was seven, right before her eyes. She'd told a man she met at a skanky bar outside of Alamagordo that her uncle had diddled her for three years, from the time she was seven (a lie), and the man had taken her back to his foul-smelling motel room and laid her down on the bed and said, "Now tell old Terry how your uncle did you."

Sometimes it makes her smile, thinking about old Terry waking up the next morning with a concussion and his car and wallet stolen.

She told Jeremy she was twenty-three, which was the truth, and he told her he was twenty-four, though he seems much older. Still, she has no reason not to believe him. And what do ages matter anyway?

If Jeremy had asked her what she was doing there on the side of I-10 in the middle of a field of yellow wildflowers, she would have told him the truth: she'd been driving for seven hours and needed to pee so badly her vision was blurring. But he didn't ask. He pulled over and jogged toward her and then stopped and said, "There you are."

"Here I am," she said. It didn't hurt that he was handsome, and that the sun was going down in a particularly spectacular way, and that she wasn't headed anyplace in particular, and that she hadn't eaten in almost twenty-four hours. The mountains in the distance were prehistoric creatures that could rise up and stomp them both. She had no problem leaving old Terry's crappy Datsun on the side of the road and getting into Jeremy's white pickup truck. He took her to a truck stop and bought her a BLT and then to K-Mart for shoes and underwear and a bathing suit.

That was three weeks ago.

"Sink Drip," she says to the cat, which is still sprawled on the floor, eyes closed. She wishes he would be a little bit more attentive.

"Moldy Shower," she says, and sighs. It's getting old, living in crappy motel rooms. Soon, they'll have enough money to buy someplace nice, maybe in the mountains. "Which mountains?" she'd asked, and Jeremy said, "Any of them. All of them."

She turns on the television. "Stone Phillips," she says. The cat's toes and whiskers twitch, in some kind of cat-dream. She leans down next to his ear. "Get it," she whispers. "Catch that mouse. Good boy."

The first car she'd ever stolen, when she was eighteen, belonged to her landlord—hers and Tim's. Tim was her husband, a thirty-eight-year-old slightly retarded janitor she'd met at the Catty Shack Catfish House in Tupelo, Mississippi. He was so charming that at first you didn't realize he was retarded. She'd married him because she was tired of living in a trailer with Ilene, a community college student who shot up heroin with her Western Civ book propped on her knees.

But after a couple of months of married life, she realized she'd had enough; she'd gotten fired at Catty Shack for slapping Tim's face in front of customers and calling him a fucking retard. The worst part of all that was that then Tim had started to cry. He threw his mop on the floor and ran out the door, got in his truck, and a day later he still hadn't come back.

She was standing at the kitchen window, eating a peanut butter and butter sandwich and staring across the yard at Mr. Harvey, the landlord, when she got the idea. Mr. Harvey kept trying to save her and Tim, coming to the door with pamphlets and tiny green New Testaments. His car, a Chevy Malibu, was parked as usual in the driveway, coated yellow with the pollen that blew all through northern Mississippi that time of year. He was out on his front porch, setting for a spell (as he called it; he was always trying to get Donna to set for a spell with him) with an old black lady who was nearly as crazy as he was. Donna had taken him for a racist, an ex-Klan member perhaps (he reminded her of her daddy), and so this friendship surprised and confused her. She liked to have people figured out.

Then Mr. Harvey and the old black lady stood up and started heading down the street, chatting intently. Even he had a friend. And there she was, eighteen years old, married to a retard, fired from a catfish restaurant, and there didn't seem to be a good reason *not* to walk up onto Mr. Harvey's back porch—it smelled like boiled vegetables and grease and tobacco—and take the car keys from his kitchen table.

She left a note: *I need this to do the Lord's work, will return it to you in 2 days, please do not call the police. GOD BLESS YOU.*

Then she found some money, too—in a sock in his underwear drawer (just like her daddy, after all)—and took off for the West, where anything could happen.

%

It was a hundred and six degrees today, according to the Weather Channel, and even at seven in the evening the heat comes off the asphalt in waves. "Why is it so smoggy and suffocating here?" she'd asked Jeremy. "I thought California was supposed to be sunny and beachy and fun, with celebrities all over the place."

"This here's the Inland Empire," he said. Whatever that meant; it sounded like something out of *Star Wars*. They'd driven past charred hillsides, palm trees burnt up like match heads. And yet people live here; they even come here on vacation. The Carrows across the parking lot is full of families: weary-looking mothers; stern, sunburned fathers; cranky children. They take up all the benches and fill up the vestibule.

Her pickup order isn't ready yet, so she stands at the brochure stand and flips through the Area Attractions: Joshua Tree National Park, Death Valley, the Hollywood Walk of Fame, Disneyland. Donna didn't tell Jeremy this, but she actually wouldn't mind going to Disneyland; she might actually enjoy it. But Jeremy has a low tolerance for people—except for her, of course. Yesterday, when they first arrived and checked in, they'd come here for lunch and Jeremy had been so annoyed that he'd handed her a twenty and told her to get something to bring back to the room.

"Excuse me," says someone. "Ma'am?" A large man in khaki shorts and a Van Halen tour T-shirt is standing up, pointing to a place on a bench. "Why don't you have a seat?"

"Thank you!" she says. "I appreciate that."

People could be so kind; that's one thing she's just beginning to understand about the world since she met Jeremy. Even the sweaty, tired-looking families around her seem like they get along; nobody's crying or smacking anyone; no one's kneeled down whispering threats in anybody's ear.

When she picks up her order finally, she looks back at the khaki-pants man on the way out the door; he's telling a little girl something that's making her laugh. Yes, people aren't so bad after all, and they don't expect you to be bad, either.

That's the thing. They don't expect you to be bad. It's amazing, she thinks—walking across the parking lot, pocketknife clutched between her knuckles—that in this day and age, people will just let you into their houses, that they will look out their peepholes and see two complete strangers standing there, and then pull the door open.

That's what Mrs. Jarvis had done. She had greeted them with an expression of confusion and expectation, as if they had been standing there holding gift-wrapped boxes. "Yes?" she had said, and that's when Jeremy (who had gotten her name from the mailbox) said, "I'm sorry to bother you, but is Mr. Jarvis home?"

"No?" the woman answered, as if this were a quiz show and she wasn't certain what she'd won but knew—knew—that she'd won something. "Is this about the boat?" she said then (and Donna nearly laughed out loud—a boat!), and Jeremy said, without missing a beat, "Yes, it is."

"I'm sorry, but we already sold that," Mrs. Jarvis said, smiling. "Thanks for coming by, though."

The plan wasn't to go inside; the plan was to get a sense of the place, see if there was anything worth stealing and come back for it later.

"Can I use your bathroom?" Donna said then. She could practically feel Jeremy's heart beating harder; the heat radiating from him almost made her dizzy.

The truth was, she had briefly forgotten about the plan. She suddenly wanted to see inside the house; she wanted to know if it was full of votive candles and Hummels, and if there was a room where everything—the furniture, the carpet—was covered in clear plastic like there was in her grandmother's home—the entire living room forbidden entry by anyone other than "company," whom she never saw.

She wanted to see if there was a bathroom cabinet full of pill bottles and if there were razor blades under the sink, and if the whole house smelled of disinfectant and Bengay.

And Mrs. Jarvis had just kept smiling. "Please," she said, "won't you come in?"

%

Jeremy's truck isn't there yet, but that's fine. "Here I am, Kitty-Kitty," she announces, opening the door. "Did you miss me?"

And the cat did miss her, because he comes leaping up on the bed like a dog to meow at her, welcoming her back.

She'd left the television on to keep him company. Donna loves cable TV, but Jeremy thinks it's dangerous. Last night, they had fallen asleep watching *Law and Order*, the cat curled up at the foot of their bed, and had woken up to some espionage movie.

Jeremy had jumped out of bed, saying, "Shit! Shit! We shouldn't have done that!"

"Done what?"

"Left the TV on all night. Fuck." Then he told her that all the stuff that had been on all night long had seeped into their subconscious, and they had no idea what it might have done to them, what kind of bad ideas and thoughts might have gotten into their brains. He grabbed the TV guide and they saw it had been a *Law and Order* marathon and he was even more pissed off.

"Better than *Golden Girls*," she'd said. "We might've woken up thinking we were horny old ladies." He didn't think that was funny.

Jeremy likes watching nature programs and documentaries about haunted houses. He told her that when he was a little boy, he'd seen a ghost appear to him in his bedroom mirror and tell him that his grandfather was about to die. "And three days later, he did. He wasn't even sick!"

And after that he'd had "the gift"—he didn't specify exactly what the gift was, just that it made him realize when something was right (like when he saw her by the side of the road with the wildflowers) or wrong (like not having a name for the cat).

She knows Jeremy wants to keep the cat, because on the way home after they found him, Jeremy had stopped at Wal-Mart—leaving her and the kitty (Biscuit? Muffin?) in the car with the air conditioner running—and came back with a litter box, litter, a ball full of catnip, and a bag of expensive, veterinarian-recommended chow made with salmon and spinach. "Nothing but the best for Whoosits," he said.

"Maybe we should call him Bluebell," she suggested. "Because of the blue bell around his neck. It's kind of obvious, but it's cute."

Then Jeremy frowned and didn't say anything until they got back to their motel room. They set the cat on the floor and he immediately lay down and began purring.

"Bluebell likes us," she said.

"His name isn't Bluebell," Jeremy said. "I think you know that. It doesn't fit."

And he was right; it didn't. This cat was stronger and bigger than a Bluebell. He was more of a . . . what?

"I don't like not knowing his name," Jeremy said, later that evening when they were eating Chinese takeout and watching a special on the Roman ghosts of Yorkshire. "It's bad luck. Not knowing something's name is like having a bad spirit floating around. Until we know what to call him, we won't be safe." He took a bite of egg roll. "Three days, and if we don't have a name for him, he's history."

Then he closed his eyes and sniffed the air, which he did sometimes, as if he could sense things coming from miles, days, even weeks away. Once he'd done this—after a job in Sedona—and said, "Trouble. We've gotta get the hell out of here." They'd packed up that night and driven up to Utah, and they hadn't had any trouble at all.

"Three days," Jeremy repeated. "And that's pushing it."

%

At nine-thirty, when Jeremy hasn't come back yet, Donna eats her chef's salad and gives all the ham to the cat, who rubs his head against her hand again and again even when there's nothing left. He knows that if she had more, she would give it to him. "You're a smart cat," she tells him. (Einstein?) Then she thinks: Maybe he doesn't want anything. Maybe he's just being nice.

Outside her window, there's the sound of a family walking down the pavement toward their room, a little boy whining about his sunburn, a mother telling him she warned him, didn't she? The voices get fainter, then a door opens and slams shut.

Before her daddy ran off and her mother went crazy and Donna (Lacey Love) went to live with her grandmother in Jackson—in the house with all the plastic on the furniture—they had all gone on a family trip to Vicksburg. "This field was running with blood," her daddy said. "Right where we're standing." Her mother had sighed and trembled. Her grandmother had refused to get out of the car. She had wanted to go to Dollywood.

Donna peeks out the window. The parking lot is nearly half empty; the fortunate families are staying down the street at the Holiday Inn or the Ramada. She steps out into the hot desert air, the pavement warm beneath her bare feet.

"You have a real knack for this kind of thing," Jeremy had told her—the way she's able to scan an entire parking lot and know which car is unlocked, or which trunk is not latched. "I'm good at guessing," she told him. "I'm lucky."

And she's lucky again tonight, locating a red Honda Civic with a piece of fabric—a beach blanket—sticking out of the trunk. The laptop is right on top—asking to be stolen, really—and she digs around a little more and finds some backpacks that don't interest her, and some AAA tour books, and some sun visors. She closes the trunk carefully and quietly. Before she met Jeremy, she would have taken the car and driven away, just because she could, but she hasn't wanted to do that in weeks. She's not sure she even could anymore.

“We’re not bad people,” Jeremy had told her. “We’re just getting by in a world that’s fucked us over.”

When she asked him how the world had fucked him over, he’d sighed and his eyes had gotten damp, and he’d held her and stroked her hair—as if to say all that didn’t matter, now that he’d found her.

She takes the laptop inside and places it on the nightstand. Inside the nightstand, she knows, is the ubiquitous Bible; it’s as if it’s the same one, following them from town to town, wanting something. She thinks of Mr. Harvey, can almost imagine him sneaking into the rooms and placing them furtively in drawers, convinced that he’s saving the world. But she knows it’s more complicated than that. Her mother thought she was saved, even when she was taking her clothes off in the middle of Wal-Mart, even when the doctor was giving her a shot in the arm to keep her from pulling out all her hair.

Donna has Jeremy, and that’s better than salvation.

%

“Good old Mrs. Jarvis,” Jeremy had said, in a playful, affectionate way, when they were standing in her living room. He was tapping his gun against his palm, thoughtfully, though there was nothing really to think about.

“I’m not old,” Mrs. Jarvis said. “I’m only forty-seven. I have a daughter at Bryn Mawr. My husband is dead. I’m the only person she has left.”

Donna had drifted through the house, which was bright and sunny and smelled nothing at all like disinfectant. It smelled like flowers. There was no fancy “company” room. The bathroom was green and pink, with a shower curtain of plastic pink flowers. The tub was empty, of course—no old lady lying there with a razor blade beside her, her eyes closed under the red water.

There was a lime tree growing in black dirt. The limes were hard and small but she took two of them anyway and put them in her pocket. She wondered if the daughter at Bryn Mawr had played in this garden as a little girl, if she’d had tea parties and cut up little limes for her dolls. Donna—back when she was Lacey Love—had made dolls out of her mother's stockings, had set them around the card table and given them Dixie cups of cold Sanka.

Later, when her grandmother took her to the hospital for a visit, her mother would hold her on her lap—even though she was getting too big for that—and sing a song from her own childhood: *Donna, Donna, where have you gone? Where have you gone?*

The gunshot came as if from far away—a distant *pop*, like a toy, and she wondered vaguely if the Bryn Mawr girl would come back here and pack up her own toys, and where she would go, and if she had someone who loved her the way Jeremy loved Donna.

Jeremy stuck his head out the screen door. "Let's hit the road," he said. "Maybe get some Wendy's on the way."

That's when the black cat dashed out the door, blue collar jingling. One of his paws had blood on it.

"There you are," Jeremy said, and scooped him up.

"Cutie," said Donna. "Let's take him with us."

"He's ours," said Jeremy.

%

She must have fallen asleep. When she hears the door open, the cat (Rex? Blossom?) is curled up next to her, on Jeremy's pillow.

"Aww," says Jeremy. "So, what'd you come up with?"

"Where were you?"

"I had a hard time finding a place. Damn guard dogs everywhere, and alarms and shit like that. I couldn't get a break. It was like an omen or something. Bad luck." He looks at the cat. "That's how I know you didn't come up with a name for him."

"Noodle," she tells him, sitting up and rubbing her eyes. Jeremy gives her a long look.

"I think you know that his name isn't Noodle."

"He looks like a noodle! Sort of. Doesn't he?"

But Jeremy is right. Noodle is wrong.

"Maybe the name of a famous person," she suggests. "Or a movie character. Like Clyde, of Bonnie and Clyde. Or maybe Billy the Kid. Or Sundance."

Jeremy is shaking his head. Daylight is leaking under the thick orange curtains, staining the carpet with smears of brightness.

"Potsie!" she says, and laughs. "Or maybe Cousin Oliver."

"Nope," says Jeremy, and moves closer to the bed, where the cat is sprawled blissfully on the pillow, one yellow eye barely visible. He rubs the cat on its stomach, and the cat stretches even further, his back legs twitching.

"Let's just keep him," Donna whispers, but Jeremy already has the cat by the neck, is squeezing with both hands while the cat (Inky! Frodo!) flails and twists and opens his poor little mouth and waves his paws in the air, his back legs frantically clawing at Jeremy's hands, until finally Donna looks away, sobbing, and there's a *crack*, and when she looks again, Jeremy is holding the limp cat on his lap, petting it. The tops of his hands are bleeding.

She watches as Jeremy picks up the animal and carries it outside; she hears something thud into the dumpster outside their room, and then Jeremy reappears and heads into the bathroom to wash his hands.

"Are you going to get ready?" he asks her.

She doesn't answer.

"Donna?"

"I don't feel like a Donna anymore," she admits, and something in Jeremy's eyes goes dark and bright and dark again. "I think I feel like a Joan," she tells him quickly, but as soon as she says it she knows it's wrong; she's not a Joan, any more than she's a Lacey Love or a Sunshine or a Donna.

Donna, where did you go?

"Agnes?" she says, but that's not right, either.

"Linda," Jeremy says, coming toward her, and she can see it in his eyes, how badly he wants that to fit, but it doesn't. "Betty," he says, holding one of her hands in both of his own. "Amber. Millicent. Penny."

"Helen," she whispers back. "Cynthia, Regina, Anne."

Anthony

The ghost had gotten inside her daughter like a tapeworm and refused to come out. How had it happened? Was it something Cindy ate? Something in the water? The water in Boardtown, Alabama, was bad, everybody knew it; Nia usually bought bottled water at Wal-Mart but this week she'd been cheap, she'd been lazy, she hadn't wanted to haul all those bottles to the car. And now a ghost inhabited her child and wouldn't be budged.

Her husband, Jake, blamed it on Nia; *he* would never let something like this happen to their child; he would have beat the crap out of that ghost before it could get near his daughter. Nia didn't argue with him. She had been planning to leave him for months. He had a temper and she was almost positive he was screwing the waitress at Longshots, the bar where they'd met seven years ago and where he spent more and more of his time, sometimes not coming home until three-thirty in the morning. The bar closed at two, so what the hell was he doing until three-thirty? Not that she cared.

"It's because you don't make her take a bath every day," he said. "It's because you feed her macaroni and cheese from a box. That shit is horrible for a kid."

"How the hell do you know what I feed her? Since when are you around for any meals anyway?" Sometimes she argued with him just because she wanted to see how close he would get to hitting her. He'd done it once and she'd threatened to take Cindy and leave if he ever did it again, and now when he clenched his fists and got up in her face, she stared right back at him and said, "I dare you," and watched him use every ounce of his strength not to bash her in the nose. She wanted to laugh every time, because she was leaving him anyway.

It must have happened on Tuesday night, when—yes, she *had* forgotten to give Cindy a bath after her dinner of mac and cheese from a box. Nia had been on the computer finishing up her homework for Accounting 101, a ridiculously easy course taught by a man who looked like he was twelve. Still, it was hard to keep up when you had a child and a full-time job at Blockbuster. She wanted more for herself, and just when she thought she was getting somewhere—didn't it figure—something like this had to happen.

The kindergarten teacher, Miss Missy, had been the one to take Cindy to the nurse's office on Wednesday morning. Miss Missy had seen many things in her life: she'd seen a crop-dusting plane fall out of the sky above the cotton fields behind her house; she'd woken up in the middle of the night to see her baby sister in the arms of a Skunk Ape (startled by Missy's cries, it had dropped the baby back in the crib and fled out the window); she'd seen the spirit of her lynched grandfather swinging from a tree.

So when tiny, blonde Cindy Morgan's stomach shouted, "Time to party!" in the voice of a young black male, Miss Missy kept her wits. The children were just down for their naps, and Miss Missy was in the process of cleaning up the Nilla wafer crumbs and milk cartons from snack time. She detested Nilla wafers, but the children loved them. Those, and Fig Newtons. Her own childhood in Tuscaloosa had been filled with chitlins—which stunk halfway down the street—and pork barbeque. She and her sister munched happily on fried pig snouts ("*Snoots*," her Mawmaw called them) after school, watching *The Munsters* and *Gilligan's Island* until their mother came home from work.

"Time to party!" said Cindy Morgan's belly, and the other children turned on their mats and yawned, and Cindy sat up and said, in her own baby-voice, "Miss Missy, I feel funny."

Miss Missy walked briskly across the room, knelt, and felt Cindy's forehead.

"I ain't sick, I'm dead," said the voice from Cindy's stomach. Or maybe it was more the solar plexus. It was hard to be sure.

Nurse would know.

*

Nurse felt dread when she saw Miss Missy marching Cindy Morgan into her office. She had noticed the girl earlier that month, being dropped off twenty minutes late in a rusty orange El Camino by a woman in a too-short skirt and too-high heels. Mothers like this were usually bad news; they usually had boyfriends with tattoos and motorcycles, boyfriends who didn't like little children. Or liked them too much.

Please, no bruises, Nurse prayed silently, and looked Miss Missy in the eye, as if daring her to say what Nurse least wanted to hear.

"Cindy here is having stomach . . . difficulties," said Miss Missy. She put her hands on Cindy's shoulders and said, "Sweetheart, Nurse will take care of you, okay?"

"Okay," said Cindy Morgan, and then Miss Missy spun on a heel—Nurse admired Miss Missy's ability to wear heels—and was gone.

Nurse leaned down and looked into Cindy's pale blue eyes. "Does your tummy hurt?" she asked, smiling, relieved that her worst fears had not come to pass. Two weeks ago, she had lifted up Timmy Maxwell's Pooh Bear shirt to discover cigarette burns around his nipples. A woman from Social Services had arrived to lead a sobbing Timmy out to a big white car. Nurse hadn't seen him since.

She led Cindy into the examination room and helped the girl up onto the paper-covered table. "Can you tell me where it hurts?"

"I feel like dancin'," said the voice of a young black man. Then he laughed, a joyful sound that made Nurse almost laugh, too.

Cindy frowned. "He wants to dance," she said. "But I don't."

"Well, now, let's just take a look." Nurse lifted up Cindy's pink Care Bears shirt and placed her stethoscope on her white stomach.

"It's cold," Cindy said, and then giggled.

"Breathe deeply," said Nurse. "That's a good girl. Will you lie down for me, sweetheart?"

Cindy lay her head back on the paper pillow and closed her eyes. Nurse touched around her belly button very gently, trying to locate the source of the strange male voice. She had never encountered anything like this before, had never read about it in nursing school or on any of the nursing blogs she looked at every evening while she ate a Lean Cuisine in front of her computer.

"Hello?" said Nurse. "Is anybody there?"

"*I'm* here," said the young male voice. "I'm here, and I'm ready to party. Hell yeah!" He laughed again, and Nurse couldn't help smiling. Then he said, gently, "You're a damn good nurse," and Nurse felt herself blushing and had to turn away and clear her throat.

%

Nia was at work that Wednesday afternoon, scanning in new DVDs of some violent Mexican movie she couldn't pronounce, when she got the phone call from the nurse's office. Then she had to bribe Sherry to cover for her by offering to work the weekend shift. Sherry was a sorority girl and she worked at Blockbuster because, as the poorest girl in the sorority, she needed the money but only if she could work a job that wouldn't make her seem like too much of a loser. Before Blockbuster, she had worked at McDonald's, which was humiliating, absolutely mortifying, all that grease, all those miserable single mothers she had to work with! She lasted one day because at the start of her second shift, Tad from Psi Upsilon came in and ordered hash browns and then said, "Fuck, Sherry. What are you doing here?" and Sherry took off her paper cap and yelled, "I quit!" right there. She'd hoped Tad might be so impressed by this that he'd ask her out, but he'd just laughed and asked for ketchup.

Blockbuster was better because (a) there was no grease and (b) she could watch movies all day long and (c) sometimes she could get Nia to take over the weekend shift for her so she could go out with her friends, cruise the bars—there weren't many—and meet up with boys, though not Tad, because he'd date-raped this girl Racine and everybody knew it, even though she refused to go to the campus police.

Nia always had a frazzled look about her, and her hair looked like it had been bleached too many times. Sometimes Sherry wished she could give Nia a makeover.

%

When Nia got Cindy home, she took her temperature (normal, just as the nurse had said) and tucked her into bed and brought her some chicken noodle soup.

"It's probably just a virus, sweetheart," she told Cindy, and she heard the young man sigh heavily and mutter something.

"Did you want to speak up?" Nia demanded, and the young man said, "No, ma'am," very politely. "Do you want to leave, then?" she said, and he didn't answer.

When Jake got home, Nia took him into the living room and explained, quietly, what the nurse had told her: Cindy had the ghost of a young black man living in her stomach, and he didn't seem dangerous, but they ought to keep an eye on her.

That's when Jake accused her of not feeding or bathing Cindy properly, and that's when Nia dared him to smack her.

Jake could be a good father when he put his mind to it, and he picked Cindy up from her bed and kissed her on the cheek and said, "What's this about feeling bad?"

"I'm okay now," she said.

"Who are you?" Jake demanded of Cindy's stomach. "What do you want from us?"

"Don't yell at him," said Nia. "His name is Anthony." She'd actually had a pleasant, though brief, conversation with the young man. He'd died in a car accident, but he wouldn't talk much about that except to say that people should wear their seatbelts.

"Anthony?" shouted Jake. "Make thyself known!"

"For God's sake, Jake," said Nia. "He's not a Shakespearean actor. He's just a teenaged boy."

"Can I have the television in my room?" Cindy wanted to know, and Anthony said, "Say please," and Cindy said, "Please?"

"Show some respect," Anthony said, and then didn't say anything else for the rest of the night, although he chuckled occasionally during the *Happy Days* reruns.

%

That night, Miss Missy told her new boyfriend, Hank, about Cindy Morgan.

"It must be so hard on the family," she said. "But people learn to live with things, you find ways to get by."

Hank, who taught third grade, thought Miss Missy (he just called her Missy) was the most graceful, beautiful, intelligent woman he had ever met. He loved the little gap in her teeth and he loved that she wore such sexy clothes to work, those tight pencil skirts and high heels. No jumpers and sneakers for her, like the other kindergarten teachers wore.

They had only been dating for two months but he was ready to ask her to marry him; he could picture their children playing on the swing set at his mother's house, could imagine calling, "Henry! Deanne! Time for dinner!"

Now was not the time to propose, however; Missy looked vexed. She paced the floor in her bare feet. She sat down on the sofa and put her head in her hands. The polish on her toenails was pink and the polish on her fingernails was silver. He felt his breath catch, and tried to focus.

Hank had never heard of this particular situation, but he admired Missy's ability to try to get to the bottom of things. "I think they'll be fine," he told her, and she leaned against him and closed her eyes. And even though he had transparencies to make and dioramas to grade, he stroked her head and said, "There, there," until she was snoring.

%

Nurse was at home, eating a Lean Cuisine in front of her computer and Googling "child ghosts," which did not produce the result she was looking for. "Stomach ghost," she tried, and then "haunted stomach," but, again, the results proved fruitless. Then she found herself tempted to type in the dating Web site that had gotten her here in the first place, living alone in a podunk Alabama town, so she turned the computer off. She told herself she wasn't that lonely, and if she was she should just go to sleep and not think about it.

%

Cindy's pediatrician said, "I can't vaccinate her for this, but I don't think she's in any danger."

"She's not," said Anthony.

"They're getting along pretty well," said Nia. "I hear them talking late at night sometimes."

"How long has this been going on?" the pediatrician asked, suddenly suspicious.

"Only about . . . less than a week?" Nia said. She was lying. It had been three weeks since Anthony made his appearance, but she told herself it wasn't as if Cindy was *ill.* Besides, Cindy hated the doctor. But the school nurse was scaring Nia with stories of parasites and poltergeists and wanted Cindy to take antibiotics, so Nia thought she'd better get a second opinion.

And Cindy and Anthony *were* getting along; that part was true. Last night Nia had hovered outside Cindy's door—Cindy liked to keep it closed now, even though she used to be afraid of the dark—and heard Cindy giggling, and then Anthony laughing, and then Cindy talking, Anthony replying. More giggling from both of them. What on earth did they have to say to one another, a six-year-old and a dead fifteen-year-old? Nia was tempted to hide a tape recorder under Cindy's bed, but she wasn't entirely sure how to rig it so it wouldn't click loudly when it shut off.

"How's your husband handling this?" the pediatrician asked, in low tones.

Nia rolled her eyes. "Fine," she said.

The truth was, Jake had been mad because Anthony was black. He wanted a white ghost. He wanted, specifically, Marilyn Monroe. "Or James Dean!" he'd said. "How cool would that be?"

What could you do with a man like that?

"You feel all right, don't you, Cindy-girl?" said the pediatrician, producing a green lollipop from his coat, and Cindy said, "Yes, sir, I feel fine. Thank you for asking."

"Well, now!" laughed the pediatrician. "Aren't you polite."

Nia felt stung. It was Anthony who'd taught her that.

He still sometimes said "hell" and wistfully said he wanted to party, but only when Cindy was taking a nap or preoccupied with cartoons.

"What kind of party do you want, Anthony?" Nia asked once, when they were watching TV together on the sofa. (Cindy had fallen asleep during *Dateline*; Anthony enjoyed it, as he enjoyed most of the programs Nia watched.) All she could get out of him was a sigh. He did that a lot, and it made her sad for him. It made him seem older than his years.

%

Jake thought Anthony was a riot. At first, yes, he was pissed off, and not because he was a racist, either. He just figured that if his daughter was going to have a ghost in her stomach, it ought to be someone . . . well, famous. Someone interesting. He wanted the TV news crews to come over and interview him, and interview the famous person, and maybe film the two of them together—Jake and James Dean—chatting about cars or something.

But Anthony was a cool little dude, and he cracked Jake up. One evening, when Nia was at her accounting class and Cindy was napping on the sofa (Cindy napped a lot lately), he had said, "You know how to make a hormone?"

"A what?" said Jake.

"Don't pay her."

When Jake stopped laughing, he said, "Do you—did you play any sports when you were alive? Basketball, maybe?"

"Nah," said Anthony. "I had to take care of my little brothers after school, help out my mother and shit."

"What about your dad?"

"What about him?" Anthony said bitterly.

Anthony needed a father figure, someone to talk about guy stuff with, someone to guide him in the ways of women.

"You can talk to me," Jake said. "I'm here for you."

"'Preciate it," Anthony said.

%

One night, when Cindy was sound asleep, Nia tiptoed into her daughter's bedroom and whispered, "Anthony? Are you awake?"

"I'm awake," he said. "Don't need no sleep. Just lyin' here, collectin' my thoughts."

She pulled a chair next to the bed, stroked Cindy on her pale forehead. "I'm just wondering how long you were planning on staying? Not that it isn't nice having you."

"Nice bein' here!" he cried. "I mean it. I like you people. You all right."

Nia felt relieved, then remembered why she was there. "I was just thinking," she said, "that there might be something you want, or need . . . something to, I don't know, help you go toward the light? Somehow?"

He didn't say anything.

"Don't you have parents wondering where you are? I know that if I were dead and Cindy was also dead, and I didn't get to see her, I'd worry."

"Dunno," he said, and gave one of his sad little sighs.

Then, because she had spent lunch hour crying in the Blockbuster bathroom, and because she was failing her ridiculously easy accounting class, and because here was this sad boy lost and far from home, she broke down and wept. "I'm sorry," she sniffled, "I'm sorry if it's my fault."

"It ain't," Anthony said gently. "Shit just happens."

"I'm thinking I should leave Jake," she admitted, and cried a little harder.

"Aw, man, that sucks," Anthony said. "Whaddya gonna do that for anyways?"

"He's a terrible husband," she said. "He's never home, and I know he's screwing some slut he met at Longshots! Sorry," she added, and blushed. Sometimes it was hard to remember that Anthony was barely more than a child himself.

"Seems like he's home all the time," Anthony said, and Nia realized it was true. Just last night, she had come home from class to find Jake, Cindy, and Anthony playing Candyland on the kitchen table. "Where's the babysitter?" she had demanded, and Jake said, "I sent her home," and moved his marker toward Gumdrop Mountain.

And two nights ago, Jake had offered to help cook dinner.

"Because I'm such a terrible cook, is that it?" she'd snapped, and he'd kissed her on the cheek and said no, he just wanted to help out.

"I only married him because I was pregnant," she whispered. Anthony didn't say anything, and so after a moment she gave Cindy's tummy a pat and tiptoed from the room.

⁂

Miss Missy enjoyed having Anthony in the classroom. He was never disruptive, and the other students listened to him. If anyone got too rambunctious—if Gino pulled Caroline's hair, or Dana hit Rachel—Anthony would say, "Have some respect!" and they would stop.

You expected ghosts to be trouble, but Anthony was a joy, and this is what she wrote on his progress report. But it concerned her that he wasn't getting the kind of education he needed. *Anthony could go very far*, she wrote, *if he had the opportunity.*

On Cindy's report, she wrote: *Needs to speak up more in class.* Then, because she liked the girl, she added: *Cindy is a sweet child, and she knows most of her numbers.*

At the parent-teacher conference, she suggested to Cindy's parents that Anthony needed a tutor. Just because he was dead and stuck inside a six-year-old's body didn't mean he should be denied a good education. Everyone had things to overcome.

"We're all," she said, "differerently-abled, in our own way."

"We'll look into it," Cindy's father said. "We only want the best for him."

"You're good parents," Miss Missy said. "Anthony is lucky he found you."

%

Their usual babysitter was busy, so when Jake asked Nia on a date ("Remember dates?" he asked), they had to scramble to find someone else. Nia immediately thought of Sherry.

"He doesn't need a babysitter," Jake had insisted.

"No, but she does," said Nia.

Really, thank God she was the responsible parent around here. Thank God at least one of them was watching out for their daughter.

"Will you be nice to the babysitter?" Nia asked Cindy, and Cindy yawned and said, "Okay," in a tiny voice.

"That's my girl," Nia said.

%

Sherry was surprised by how neat Nia's house was; she'd been expecting something much dumpier and red-necky—maybe a Confederate flag and a beat-up pickup truck in the driveway—but it wasn't bad at all, certainly no trashier than some of the fraternity houses she'd been to. There were candles and potpourri in the living room and framed pictures of Cindy as a baby, Nia holding her and smiling at the camera, looking almost beautiful. Most surprising of all, Nia's husband was a hottie. How did someone like her end up with someone like him?

Nia had led Sherry through the house (she caught a glimpse of the master bedroom, of the neatly made bed and the big pillows), ending up in the kitchen and saying, "Here's all the emergency numbers, poison control, you know the drill. I'll have my cell phone with me. Help yourself to the Hot Pockets in the freezer. Cindy already had her dinner."

"Is there anybody else I should call if I can't get through? Cindy's grandparents or something?" Sherry didn't care about Cindy's grandparents; she was just nosy.

"Grandparents are dead," Nia said, and then frowned as if something had just occurred to her. "Actually, there is someone you could contact." That's when she told Sherry about Anthony. "He's been quiet the past few hours, but he'll probably be around later on. He likes to watch *Dateline*. He's really good with kids, and he's smarter than you'd think for someone so young. I just didn't feel comfortable leaving her alone, you know? Because they do share the same body, so if she fell down or something, there's nothing he could really do."

Sherry nodded. "Gotcha," she said. She couldn't wait to call up Tad—he wasn't her boyfriend, exactly, but he had started hanging around the store lately, and a couple of times they made out in the back room. She gave him DVDs from the sale rack—who was going to notice if they were gone anyway? But she didn't think that was the only reason he liked her. He told her Racine made up the date-rape stuff, and she believed him because it was exactly the sort of thing Racine would do.

Cindy was lying on the floor, coloring in a My Pretty Pony coloring book. Sherry sat down next to her. She was terrible with kids, but she needed the money, so what could she do? "Hey there," she said, in a fake-sounding voice. "Whatcha got there?"

"My Pretty Pony," Cindy said. "Do you want to color with me?"

The girl looked pale and her eyes were bleary.

"Um, not really," Sherry said. She'd read somewhere that it was important to be honest with kids. Was that in her Marriage and the Family class? She'd pretty much snoozed through that one. That class was full of brainless debutantes who wanted to be married by the time they were twenty.

"Okay," Cindy sighed, and went back to listlessly running a blue crayon over the page.

With Cindy occupied, Sherry made herself comfortable on the sofa and took out her cell phone.

"Who you callin'?" It startled her, that voice coming out of Cindy's stomach.

"Tad," she said, and the voice laughed as if that was the funniest thing in the world.

"Tad! Tad ain't a name. *Tad*. Oh, *Tad*." He was imitating a British voice now. "I *say* now, Tad, tally ho and all that."

"Cut that out. You don't even know him. He's in a fraternity and he's really cute and really cool."

"Yeah, he sounds like a real—" he lowered his voice. "A real dick weed, you know?"

"You don't know shit," she said. Then something occurred to her. "Do you? I mean, can you see what he's doing right now?"

"Jackin' off," he said. "But he sure ain't thinking of you."

Sherry didn't buy it. "You're just being a jerk."

Cindy gave a loud sigh and put her head down on her coloring book.

"That's right sweetie," said Sherry. "You take a nap now."

Sherry told Anthony about Tad, about how he came to the store and she gave him DVDs and how they kissed in the back room, and how he didn't date-rape Racine after all.

"He's using you," Anthony said. "That is typical male behavior, is what that is. He ever take you on a date?"

"No," she said. "But so what?"

"You know so what," he said. "You can do better."

"I can?" said Sherry. She felt herself getting weepy. It was true, everything Anthony was saying. "I want him to like me!" she wailed. "I want him."

"Why?"

"Because," she said, and started crying again. Finally she managed to whisper, "Because he doesn't want me."

They talked and talked, and Anthony told her jokes, and she forgot all about the Hot Pockets and watching TV and she even forgot about calling Tad. When she heard the keys jingling in the lock a little before midnight, she quickly scooped up snoring Cindy and tucked her into bed. When Nia peeked her head in, Sherry was stroking Cindy's cheek and saying, "You're such a sweetheart, such a sweetheart."

%

Sometimes Nurse poked her head into Miss Missy's classroom and said, "Can I please speak to Cindy?" She felt it was important to keep close tabs on the girl, make sure she was doing all right.

Also, she enjoyed talking to Anthony. She even found herself telling him about Rick, the man she'd met online, the man she had moved to Alabama for and who had broken her heart. She'd met him in a chat room for certain personality types, and after chatting for a few months he'd bought a plane ticket to Boston. Nurse was forty-two and Rick was thirty-six, and—she didn't tell Anthony this part—the sex was the best she'd ever had. Her ex-husband, Denny, had been clumsy. Two months later she'd quit her job at Boston General and moved to Alabama for love. Or, more accurately, for sex—again, she didn't tell Anthony this, only that "I really thought I'd found my soul mate, the man I'd spend the rest of my life with."

But after supporting him for six months—paying his rent, buying dog food for his ridiculous Doberman—she'd had enough. Soon, she would make her way back east, but she had used up all her savings and she had to get her head on straight. "So here I am," she said, "and I have to tell myself I'm doing some good with my life, that I'm making some kind of difference, otherwise I'll go nuts." Then she told him—because he was such a good listener—about the poverty and the abuse and the kids who came to her office twice a week for baths because they had no hot water at home. It almost broke her heart, she was almost ready to give up, and then—

"And then?" said Anthony.

"And then you came along," she said, and patted Cindy on the knee.

%

Miss Missy found Cindy hiding in the coat cubby, crying and pounding on her stomach.

"Cindy sweetheart, what is it?"

Cindy continued pummeling her stomach with her tiny fists. "I hate you!" she sobbed. "Go home."

Miss Missy took her by the hand and led her down the hall to Nurse, who gave Cindy a red lollipop and told her she shouldn't hit people.

"Yes, ma'am," Cindy said weakly.

"I'm sure you didn't mean to hurt Anthony's feelings."

"Yes, ma'am," Cindy whispered.

※

The pediatrician said, "She'll eat when she's hungry."

"But it's been two whole days," Nia said. "Her teacher says she won't even drink her milk during snack time."

"You feeling all right, Cindy-girl?" said the pediatrician.

"She's fine," said Anthony.

"You're looking out for her, young man, aren't you?" said the pediatrician. "Keep it up. Maybe you-all should take her out for a cheeseburger. You feel like a cheeseburger, Cindy?"

Cindy shrugged.

"She doesn't have a fever," the pediatrician said. "But if she's feeling poorly, let her stay home from school a couple of days."

※

The tutor came for three hours in the morning and taught Anthony history, English, and math. Since Cindy couldn't stay awake long enough to read, the tutor read the textbooks out loud to Anthony and then asked him questions. The Socratic Method. The tutor was a twenty-nine-year-old named Mark who was majoring in Special Education and needed the money to pay tuition. Last year he'd tutored a blind girl, but she was kind of a bitch—he hated to admit it, but it was true—and so it was a pleasure to have a tutee as enthusiastic and intelligent as Anthony. He was lazy at times—but what fifteen-year-old wasn't?

Mark read him "A Good Man Is Hard to Find," and Anthony laughed at the beginning, at the grandmother and the cat and the bratty kids, and then he got quiet and then he started saying, "Oh, no way, man. No way." After Mark finished, Anthony said, "I didn't see that coming. Man. That was a damn good story. What else you got?"

Sometimes Mark stayed for four hours instead of three, but he told Nia not to worry about paying him for the extra hour.

%

"Anthony honey," said Nia, spooning chicken noodle soup into Cindy's mouth. "You have to go." It broke her heart to say it.

"Got nowhere *to* go," he said. "I like you people."

"Well, Cindy's feeling bad and I hate to say it, but I think it's because of you."

"Maybe she has the flu," said Anthony, sulkily. "Ain't my fault if she has the flu."

"It *might* be the flu," Nia allowed. "But I don't think so."

Anthony didn't answer. He didn't say anything the rest of the day, or the next, or the day after that. Cindy got out of bed and lay on the floor in her nightgown, coloring.

One evening at dinner, Jake said, "Anthony, you want to watch *Die Hard* with me?" No response. "God damn it," said Jake. "I'm going out for a little while."

Alone in the house with Cindy, Nia felt a depth of emptiness she hadn't felt in months. When Cindy crawled into her lap with a Berenstain Bears book, Nia said, "Not now honey, Mommy's tired." Then, feeling guilty, she said, "Oh, okay." But she couldn't muster up much enthusiasm.

It wasn't that she was upset that Jake had left, that he had probably gone to Longshots to meet up with the waitress. She felt relieved. She had realized, over the past few months, with Jake always around—always wanting to spend time with her, always after her in bed—that not only did she not love him, she never could. His hands were rough; he had a dumb sense of humor. *He's a good man*, she told herself; *he's a good father*.

She had married him because she couldn't think of a better alternative. It was hard being a single mother; her own mother had raised her and they had nearly starved, had slept in the car for two weeks, had shoplifted milk and hot dogs.

She and Jake had hardly even known each other; they had slept together more than dated; she was missing her ex when he came along. She'd had too much to drink.

She used to tell herself that she could fall in love with him, if he'd give her the chance. But she couldn't. She never would.

%

Miss Missy noticed that Cindy Morgan was losing her blank, haunted look. Her eyes were no longer lined with black circles. She was drinking her milk, and she played patty-cake.

But the class was in shambles.

Without Anthony in the classroom, Dana hit Rachel and Gregory pushed Benjamin off the swings and Wendall gave Marty a black eye. Veronica cried in the corner during story time and kicked anyone who got near her.

"Children need role models," Miss Missy said to Hank.

"Our children will be happy," he said, and Miss Missy was so surprised she couldn't think of a response.

%

Nurse treated the children's cuts and took their temperatures, and she called Social Services when a third grader named Reggie showed up in her office with welts on his back.

Sometimes she stayed awake until three a.m., emailing men and telling them she was thinner, blonder, and happier than she actually was. Sometimes she told them she would meet them, but she never did.

%

Jake started staying out until three-thirty every night, and when he got home he passed out on the sofa. One early morning Nia thought she heard him crying in his sleep, and she wished there was something she could do. But there wasn't.

She missed Anthony. She knew he was there—where else could he go?—but he refused to speak. Sometimes she could swear she heard him sniffling, just a little. It broke her heart.

And then one night when she was tucking Cindy in, Anthony said, "I miss talking to ya'll."

Nia was so happy she picked Cindy out of bed and kissed her on the stomach, which made her daughter shriek and kick and wail.

"Don't do that again," Nia said. "Do you promise?"

"I promise," said Anthony, but he had to say it twice, so Nia could hear him over Cindy's sobs.

%

It was Miss Missy who told Nurse that Cindy Morgan was no longer enrolled in school, that Cindy's mother had moved away, taking the child and leaving the father behind. He had come home from work and found them gone.

"That's too bad," said Nurse. She looked like she was about to cry. "I'll miss them."

"Yes," said Miss Missy. She was mulling over Hank's proposal and had been distracted for the past few days; there was so much risk involved, this tying of oneself to another. Things could get complicated.

Nurse was staring sullenly at the floor. Miss Missy thought of giving her a hug, of telling her everything would be fine. She wanted to reassure Nurse that she would find love someday, that she had to have faith that everything would work out for the best. She wanted to ask Nurse if she thought she was doing the right thing, marrying Hank, because things could go so wrong so fast, and you never knew what you were in for.

"They might be back," Nurse said, in a hoarse whisper. "They might."

"They might," said Miss Missy. She gave Nurse an awkward pat on the arm, then headed back to her classroom to dole out the Nilla wafers.

Grand Canyon

After his third wife left him for good, my father called to ask if I wanted to go camping in the Grand Canyon. "I don't camp," was all I could think to say. I hadn't spoken to my father in half a year. I'd answered the phone on the first ring, thinking it was either my best friend, Marcie, calling to tell me about the Journey concert, or my other best friend, Nick, calling to tell me he knew I was in love with him. I'd been expecting that phone call for months, but it hadn't come yet.

"Sure you do," my father said. "Remember that time in Virginia? When you were six?"

That was ten years ago, and I didn't remember. Downstairs, my mother was running the vacuum for the fourth time that day, making rows like miniature crops in the green carpet of the living room. It was 1984, the third week in May, the second straight week of hundred-degree temperatures.

"Where are you calling from?" I asked. Last I'd heard, he lived in Boston, which was a long way from Tucson, Arizona.

"I'm in Phoenix," he said. "Thought I'd swing down through Tucson on my way to Mexico. I'm moving to Mexico, can you imagine?"

"Why Mexico?"

"I'll tell you all about it while we're camping."

"Mexico," I informed him, "is nowhere near the Grand Canyon."

"The whole time you were growing up," he said, his voice suddenly low and serious, "I never took you to the Grand Canyon. I lived in Arizona ten years and never went to the Grand Canyon! It's nuts."

"I went with the Girl Scouts. It's a big hole."

"But I've never *been*. It's a natural goddamn wonder and I've never even *been*."

"Do you have a girlfriend in Mexico or something?" I asked, to get him to stop whining. I imagined my father wearing a sombrero and dancing with a barefoot, black-haired girl. I don't know how I came up with that scenario; all of his wives were older than him, and none were dark-haired beauties. He went for pale, lumpy women who wore no makeup. My mother—the prettiest of them all, and she wasn't pretty either—told me, not that I wanted to hear it, that he was terrible in bed. And yet I could imagine him drinking piña coladas with some beautiful Juanita.

"No girlfriend," he said.

"Drugs," I said, replacing Juanita with a sack of white powder.

"Actually, I think I can get some pretty cheap antacid medicine down there," he said. "The kind you usually need a prescription for. That's a good idea."

"I don't want to go camping with you," I told him, and placed the receiver on the hook. Two days later, he showed up anyway.

%

Today, my mother arrives at the Baltimore airport for her annual spring visit, looking gaunt yet flowery, her gray face set off by a fuchsia ruffle around her neck. My husband, Reg, and I are there to meet her, and she kisses us both and says, "I need a cigarette," and starts digging through her purse.

"You can't smoke in the airport, Mom," I tell her. "You have to wait till we're outside." She knows this perfectly well, but every year she pretends she doesn't. She took up smoking five years ago, after giving up sugar and milk products. We walk toward baggage claim, and my husband says, "How was your flight?" and my mother says, "Terrible," and then pats him on the arm as if to say she knows it wasn't his fault.

Reg and I had been married for less than a year when my father died. The day after the funeral, my mother announced that she was going to fly back to Maryland with us. "Reg can help me sell my house over the computer," she said. "I can sleep on your sofa."

Reg had never even met my mother until then, and suddenly I was saying things like, "We can convert the garage," and he was saying, "It's not a *garage*, it's a *carport*."

We decided that we'd steer her gently in the direction of condos and townhouses, but before the plane even landed she'd plastered her face to the window and said, "My God, this is ugly. Most places look okay from this high up, but not here." And she stayed for a week and went back to Tucson, still shaking her head at how I could bear to live in a place so green and humid and smoggy.

"But your father would have loved it," she admitted wistfully. They had been back together for six months when he died.

Tonight at dinner, after she's complained more about the humidity and scowled at me for not letting her smoke in the house, I watch my mother pick at her food. Her veins shine through her skin, reminding me of rivers from high above the earth, seen through clouds.

%

That hundred-degree May when I was sixteen, my father pulled up in front of our house and honked four times, then another four, until I came running outside to tell him to go away.

"Pack your stuff," he said.

I went back inside. My stuff was already packed. It had been packed for two days.

My mother stood in the middle of the living room, holding the vacuum handle, so still and dignified she could have been a Franklin Mint ceramic housewife. "I'll be fine," she said, in a way that made me know she wouldn't be. "Maybe I'll go to the movies. Or Sears or something, see if anything's on sale."

I looked at her doubtfully, half wishing she'd demand that I stay. But of course she would never do that. "I'll be fine," she said again. "Get out there and tell him to stop all that honking." She switched the vacuum back on, so I had to yell over the noise that I'd be back on Monday. "Have a good time at the movies!" I shouted, and she gave me a desperate-yet-striving-to-be-brave smile. She would use it again two years later, when I told her I was moving to the East Coast for college.

"I was about to go in there and bring you out myself," my father said good-naturedly when I got in his car. "And risk the wrath of your mother."

"She wasn't mad at all," I told him.

"You look good," he said. "Are things good?"

"I guess," I said. "Whatever that means."

We were driving down Speedway, toward the freeway, and for a moment I felt like I was seven years old, and he was taking me to my Brownie meeting. I thought of asking if he remembered driving me to Brownies but then decided against it.

"That's new," I said, indicating the Circle K on the corner of Speedway and Sixth.

"It all looks the same to me," my father said. "Don't miss the heat, that's for sure. Hopefully, Mexico'll be a little cooler. At least by the beach."

He patted my knee. My dad, always in a good mood. Mom could be screaming her head off and Dad'd just be watching TV with a smile on his face like nothing at all was the matter. He looked no older than the last time I'd seen him, four years ago, when I flew to Boston to spend Thanksgiving with him and his second wife, whose name I can't remember. The dental hygienist. By New Year's, she had left him and gone back to her ex-husband. One thing about my mother that made her different from Wives Two and Three: she didn't do the leaving.

"Why'd you decide to move to Mexico?" What I wanted to ask was, "Why'd what's-her-face leave you?" But I figured he'd get around to that eventually.

"I'm getting old," he said. "You get to a point in life where it's now or never, and you have to figure out what's most important."

"That's what you said before," I told him. "That's what you said when you left us for the dental hygienist."

My father frowned at me. "You don't remember that." I thought it was interesting that he didn't deny it. Actually, I don't know if he did say that; I was only seven and I thought it was fun to be able to sleep in the big bed with Mom, and fun to eat nothing but cookies, and fun that I didn't have to go to school because she wanted me to stay home with her and keep her company while she cried and baked. It wasn't for about two weeks that I realized I was absolutely miserable, and then I started crying all day, too. We were quite a pair, Mom and I, both of us flung across her big bed sobbing our little hearts out, then making cookies and watching *The Wonderful World of Disney* until we felt better.

But now, I thought I actually did remember him saying that; I could conjure him standing in our doorway saying, "I've reached a time in my life where I realize what's important," and tipping his hat (I must have got that from *Father Knows Best*, my father never wore a hat) and backing out the door.

By now I'd worked myself into a fit of pissed-off-edness; my insides were composed entirely of balled-up fists.

"You got dumped," I said, and he didn't deny that either.

"She was another crazy." He shook his head. "Why do I attract the crazies?"

"Mom is not a crazy," I told him, and he gave me a look that meant he didn't believe me. Or believed I didn't know what I was talking about.

"Is she doing all right with that . . . thing?" he asked.

"She's doing fine with the thing," I lied. "There's no more thing."

"Thank God," he said, sounding relieved, like *he* was the one who had to live with her.

⁂

I first realized what my mother was up to because the basement toilet overflowed. I was in the seventh grade and had three hours to myself after school before my mother got home from work. On this particular afternoon—it must have been near Christmas; I remember looking out the sliding glass door and seeing lights strung across the neighbor's pine tree—I was in the basement watching *Welcome Back Kotter* on the old black-and-white television because the good one in the living room wasn't working.

When the toilet overflowed, my first thought was to leave it and pretend I didn't know anything, and let her discover it later. Then I thought I'd be a nice, helpful daughter, so I got the plunger from upstairs and I started plunging.

At first I wasn't sure what had floated up. Then I recognized a crust of bread, with peanut butter stuck to it. My first reaction was confusion: Where did the peanut butter come from? My mother hated peanut butter, wouldn't allow it in the house, said it was nothing but lard. She'd been on a diet for the past year or so and had lost about twenty pounds. She looked good.

I cleaned up the bathroom, still baffled. At dinner, my mother stirred her steamed vegetables around on her plate and asked me how school was, and I told her fine. That night, I heard her downstairs in the kitchen, the refrigerator door opening and shutting, the microwave beeping. I'd seen enough After School Specials to suspect what she was up to, and instead of fear or disgust or even worry, I felt embarrassed: My mother, with the After School Special problem. It wasn't until later, when I'd gone to the library and checked out as many eating disorder books as I could find (the public library, not the school one), that I started thinking how gross it all was, and on top of that, she was probably going to choke to death one night on a peanut butter sandwich.

I didn't tell her I knew. I didn't tell my best friend Marcie, whose mother was dying of ovarian cancer. I didn't tell any helpful school guidance counselor; I didn't even write about it in my diary.

When Dad called, I said, "I think Mom's sick."

"What do you mean? I just talked to her, she sounds fine."

"I think she gets sick at night." I paused, unable to use any specific terminology. "In the toilet. I think she barfs and stuff."

"Ah, shit," said my father. He didn't sound particularly surprised. "Well, tell her to cut it out."

"*You* tell her to cut it out!"

Then I hung up on him, which was my usual way of saying good-bye.

Ten miles outside of Flagstaff, my father said, "Let's stop at a grocery store and get us some hamburger meat, whaddya say?"

"I say I'm a vegetarian. I say I want to eat at Denny's."

"Denny's." He said it like it was an obscenity. "Fine, then."

We went to Denny's. "She's really doing all right?" my father asked, while I was eating my cheese omelette. He was watching every bite I took. "No more funny stuff?"

"Pass the salt," I said. He stared at me, denting his hamburger bun with his fingers.

%

The day after her arrival, my mother tells me out of the blue, "I wish you'd had children."

This is a surprise. We're sitting on my front porch, having a General Foods International Coffees moment, and my mother is drinking her fourth cup of black coffee and sucking on her third cigarette. I'd just asked, "Do you feel like going to the Inner Harbor today?" and she tells me I should have children, something she's never mentioned before.

"I never knew that," is all I can think to say.

"Too late now," she says, and gums her cigarette more vigorously.

"I'm only thirty-four," I remind her. "It's not too *late*, if we even wanted kids, which we don't."

"You have a kid now, it'll be one of those whaddya-call-its. Syndrome babies." She looks sad, then brightens. "Let's go to the Inner Harbor. I need shoes."

From the abrupt way she's changed the subject, I know she isn't finished with this topic. If I try to press her—"*Why* do you want me to have children?"—she'll ignore me completely, gone conveniently deaf. But later, in a few hours or days, she'll ambush me with it again. She has a way of not acknowledging anything until she's good and ready.

When I was a freshman in college, I came home for Christmas break weighing ninety-six pounds, and all she said was, "You need a haircut." I waited and waited for her to ask me why I lost so much weight. But she never did, and I gradually realized that this was a topic of conversation that would not exist for her. Instead, she harped on me about my hair until I agreed to have it chopped at Super Cuts; then she told me I ought to wear more makeup.

When I came home for Spring Break that year, I had gained some weight, since I'd switched from puking to drinking, and then over the summer I lost it again, as I branched out into cocaine, something I'm sure my mother had never even thought of trying herself. Finally I switched from coke back to rum and coke, and there I stayed until I wrecked my car senior year and got arrested. "That was dumb," was my mother's way of showing her concern.

I met Reg in AA, something my mother knows nothing about.

As my mother and I walk through Harbor Place, which is full of kids, I try to imagine that it's my child staring at the kites in the kite store, my child whining for an ice cream, my child running pell-mell through the crowd and crashing into people. But I just can't. None of those children look like mine. Mine would be crying in a corner somewhere.

Sometimes Reg and I talk about having kids, and then we think: Yikes, do we want to give birth to someone who has *both* our fuck-up-ednesses?

Or is it fucked-up-nesses?" Reg mused the first time we talked about this.

"Either way," I said, "would suck."

%

Before my father called and asked if I wanted to go camping, this was my life: school, McDonald's with Marcie and Nick, the occasional party, where the three of us would hide out and make fun of everyone we could, sampling beer. Finally we stopped getting invited to anything. Sometimes I'd sleep over at Marcie's house and we'd make prank phone calls. Sometimes Nick would stay over too, and things weren't actually any different with him around; we still made prank phone calls, and while we painted our nails he sat on the floor writing down Dungeons and Dragons scenarios. We were young for our age, and that's why I loved them both. The first one of us to kiss a boy was Nick, but I didn't know that until years later.

My love for Nick was fueled by a combination of Danielle Steel and Sidney Sheldon, *Seventeen* and *Swank* (Marcie had a brother who kept such publications in his underwear drawer). Romance and raunch. Just like real life.

According to my mother, she and my father fell in love at first sight, gazing at each other from across a crowded Halloween party. She was dressed as Marie Antoinette, her hair piled high and covered in talcum powder; he was a cowboy in a big black hat. Although she didn't say this, I always pictured violin music, maybe doves. That's the way she made it sound, as the two of them walked toward each other across the tiled floor of some college student house in Tucson, Arizona.

But later he was a scumbag, a sleaze, "a man who would stick his dick inside anything." She's telling me this when I'm seven. I'm thinking: Shoes? The hamster cage? Milk cartons? I had no idea what she was talking about.

And she kept losing weight. Buying new clothes. If he was such a sleazebag, sticking his dick in pickle jars for all I knew, why was she making herself so pretty for him? But this was something I could not, of course, ask. And she only talked badly about my father when he wasn't around—early in the mornings, before I caught the school bus, or Saturday afternoons on our way to the grocery store.

I only heard them fight once, when I was in the second grade. It was in the middle of the night, and I had been home that day with the flu so my mother had carried the TV into my room and my father had brought home a McDonald's Happy Meal. Instead of going to sleep at my regular bedtime, I had stayed awake and watched television, turned down very low so they wouldn't hear. It was a movie I'd never seen before, about a high school girl who gets made fun of so she kills all her classmates and burns down the school.

The movie had been over for nearly an hour, but I was still lying in bed wide-awake, feeling my heart pounding in my head, my chest, my neck, my eyeballs, thinking of all that blood dripping on the girl. I had just leaned over to turn on the light when I heard my mother shout, "Go ahead and kill me. I mean it, go ahead." Then she started to cry.

"Put that down, honey," my father said. Then he said something else, but I couldn't make out what. I understood the tone of voice: patient, comforting, the voice he'd used when I fell off my training-wheeled bike and knocked out three teeth. Actually, my mother's voice reminded me of that day, too: hysterical. While my father brought me a cold towel to put on my bloody mouth, my mother had done nothing but sob in the kitchen, afraid to even look at me.

"I love you," my father was saying, and my mother cried, and during all this I turned out the light and fell, quite easily, asleep. The next morning, my father hugged me and said he was going on a long trip with a friend.

That would be wife #2, the dental hygienist, who was also married. She had long red fingernails that gouged at my gums while she cleaned my teeth.

My mother skipped work that day—she was a cashier at J. C. Penny, women's activewear—and even though I was still sick ("Too sick for school," she said, wiping her puffy eyes with the back of her hand so vigorously that her diamond ring left a thready scratch on her face), she took me grocery shopping for Pop-Tarts, cereal, Little Debbie Snack Cakes, and we got into my twin-sized bed together and watched television, surrounded by snotty tissues and crumbs.

*

"So, do you have a boyfriend?" said my father. We were back in the car, heading north. The sun was nearly down, and the mountains were a deep, shadowy blue. We were looking for a campground. The radio was getting all staticky between stations, playing a combination of "Hotel California" and a radio call-in show.

"Yeah," I said. "His name is Rick Springfield. He works in a hospital."

My father raised his eyebrows. "How old is he?"

"He's much older than me, but it doesn't matter because we're in love."

On the radio, a woman was saying, ". . . dedicate this song to my baby's father? Who's always been there for me?"

"I don't want to go camping," I said.

"Too late now." My father sounded cheerful.

"Pull over," I said then, just to see if he would. He didn't. I could see shadow-mountains rising up ahead of us and signs telling us how close we were to the Grand Canyon.

When I'd told Marcie and Nick about going camping with my dad, Marcie had seemed kind of jealous and Nick had seemed kind of sad. Which made me believe he was in love with me and wanted to spend every moment with me; and here I was being taken away for an entire weekend. He'd said, "I wish my dad would show up and take me camping," but his dad had died five years ago so what could I say to that?

"Does your mother have a boyfriend?" my father wanted to know.

It took me a minute to stop laughing.

"I'm just asking," he said.

"Yeah, right."

We were passing dinky motels with partly burnt-out signs, so they said they had "acancy" and "N V cncy."

"Why'd whoosits leave you?" I said to my father. "If you're going to make me camp, you have to at least be truthful with me. Did you cheat on her? Did she cheat on you? Is she in love with somebody younger? Is she sick of your bullshit?"

My father didn't say anything.

"Maybe she called up Mom, and Mom told her what a jerk you were, and how you left her for the dental hygienist, and maybe she decided she'd better just get out now—"

"How's this?" my father said loudly, swerving into a Motel 6 and slamming on the brakes. "We'll camp tomorrow, when you're not in such a pissy mood."

"This," I said sweetly, "will be fine."

%

When we get home from Harbor Place, my mother sighs like an invalid and says she's going to take a nap. She got depressed as we walked through the stores, and when we were having lobster bisque at Phillips, she stared down into it as if it were a crystal ball spelling out doom.

"Your father," she said, "would have loved this."

"Bisque?" I asked.

She brought a spoonful to her mouth slowly, swallowed it as if it were poison. Then she waved her hand vaguely around, at the people, the crowds moving past, the sunlight bouncing off the water.

I nodded; I knew what she meant. He would have loved feeling as if he were in the middle of something. After he'd moved to Boston he wouldn't stop talking about how much he loved the East Coast, and the water, how it made Arizona seem like a dusty old armpit.

It's Saturday, and Reg is working at the Baltimore Zoo. He's in charge of primates. They crawl around on his head and he feeds the babies with bottles, and even seeing this I never get any sort of maternal longing. "Don't you want a monkey of our own?" Reg said once, while feeding a diapered chimp. "Let's take that one," I said. "He looks just like you."

When I suggested to my mother that we go to the zoo, and Reg could show us the monkeys, she gave me a withering look and said, "I've *seen* monkeys," and that was the end of it.

Now, she's standing in the middle of the kitchen looking up at the cabinets as if they're the Matterhorn. I've brought my work into the kitchen and spread it on the table: grammar tests, one-paragraph essays. I teach remedial English at three different community colleges. My mother gives me a desperate look.

"Do you want anything?" I ask. "A snack?"

"I think I'll take a nap," she says again, and moves slowly down the hall. After a moment, I hear her go into the bathroom, and I can't help it, I stop everything, my heart feels suspended in my chest, until the toilet flushes and she comes out again. It's not that I think she's still doing it; but it's not like I can ever be really sure, either.

%

When my father and I checked into our motel room, I said, "This place stinks like a toilet."

I didn't want to think about him lying on a hammock in Mexico while my mother vacuumed obsessively and I moped around wishing someone would love me. I thought I should at least try to ruin part of his trip, at least the part that involved me.

"I don't smell anything," said my father. He lugged his backpack onto one of the twin beds.

"I want my own room." I stood there with my arms crossed, pouting like a baby. I knew it and yet still couldn't stop myself. I thought of my mother back in Tucson, roaming through the shopping malls to keep herself from throwing up, and I thought of Marcie and Nick—my only friends in the world—and self-pity clogged my throat. I almost started crying right then, but I made it into the bathroom first. I ran the water for a long time, and when I finally opened the door, the lights in the room were out and my father was a lump under the blankets.

If we were in a tent under the stars, how would that make anything better?

Lately I'd been sleeping naked, because I read in *Cosmo* that this was a way to feel sexy even when you weren't having sex. I wasn't entirely sure I wanted to have sex, ever, even though I was in love with Nick. At night, all naked beneath the sheets, I'd wonder what it would be like to have someone's skin next to mine; I'd put on my headphones and listen to the radio turned up loud, imagining that every song was about me.

I didn't sleep naked in the motel, but I considered it for about half a second. How would my father know? But it just seemed gross. I slept in my clothes, socks and all.

At a little after three a.m., I was woken by my father's snoring. Suddenly I did remember that trip to Virginia he'd mentioned, the one I thought he'd made up. We'd stayed in a cabin, and in the middle of the night he started rumbling and snorting.

"There he goes," my mother had muttered.

"Can you make him shut up?"

She shoved him until he got quiet again.

Lying there in the Motel 6 in Flagstaff, Arizona, I wondered if the women he cheated with woke up in alarm, distressed to find out that the man they'd chosen to betray their husbands with snored like a truck. I wondered if they thought, *Oh no*, or if they just shoved him, like my mother did, until he sputtered into silence.

I wondered if they just lay there for a long time, feeling guilty, letting the snores punish them.

"Shut up," I called, and for a minute he did. When he started up again, I got up and went outside, and looked up at the cold stars. The highway was silent. The Grand Canyon was just a few miles away, and I tried to imagine the Colorado River carving and carving for millions of years, but all I could see was my mother in the living room, pulling the vacuum back and forth, back and forth, forever.

By the time he woke up, I was already sitting outside drinking the complimentary coffee and eating the continental breakfast—stale blueberry muffins.

"I want to go home," I said. "I don't want to go to the Grand Canyon."

I could see his face literally fall, like something in a cartoon. I could imagine all the things he was thinking: *But we're so close, why can't you stay here and I'll go alone?* I have never felt so mean in my life.

He just nodded.

He drove me back to Tucson in near-silence, dropped me off at my mother's house, and waited until I was safely in the door before speeding away.

⁂

The night before my mother flies back to Arizona, we are alone at the kitchen table once more; Reg has gone to the movies with some of our friends. "You could have gone to the movies, too," my mother says while I set the table. "I don't mind being home by myself. I'll probably go to sleep right after dinner."

"That's fine," I tell her. "I didn't want to go anyway." This is the truth. My mother's visits always exhaust me, make me strange to myself. I find it harder to talk to Reg, less willing to be social. And then when she leaves, it takes me a few more days to be, as Reg calls it, "de-Mommed."

Tonight I just want to sit in front of the television set. I like the idea of my mother asleep in the guestroom while I watch television alone in the living room, like a babysitter. In the morning, I'll fix eggs for breakfast and then drive her to BWI, sit with her while we wait for her plane, remind her not to smoke in the airport.

"You know," my mother says, when I scoop a square of vegetarian lasagna onto her plate, "I know why you don't want to have kids. I've been reading books about it."

"You've been reading books about why *I* don't want to have kids?"

"It's because of your father," she says matter-of-factly, and puts her teeth on her fork.

I'm waiting for her to go on.

"It's because your father left us, and now you're afraid that you'll be abandoned with a child, so you don't want to have one at all."

"That's not true," I say immediately. "It's not as simple as that."

"If he had waited until you'd left for college to go off gallivanting," she continues, "you would have kids by now."

"Well, that's a theory." The vegetarian lasagna resembles soft plaster, and I have to look away, even if away is toward my mother. "But Dad wasn't the only screwed-up one, if that's what you're getting at." My mother and I are staring at each other across the kitchen table, and there's an accusation hovering between us, and a dare.

"Your father," she says sadly, breaking the spell. "I know he wasn't."

My father never made it to the Grand Canyon, or to Mexico. After he dropped me off in Tucson, he went straight back to Boston, even though wife #3 didn't want him back. He lived by himself, and while he kept offering to fly me out to visit him, for some reason I never made it.

I think he must have called my mother the day he found out he had lung cancer. He didn't tell her about it until they'd been living together for three months, and by then he only had three months left.

She never told me why she took him back, and I never asked her, but tonight I feel almost able to, or to tell her about the baby Reg and

I might have had, the one with all of our fuck-up-ednesses. We are both silent, looking at each other, but something has changed and now there's no danger. It reminds me of that day my father dropped me at home after our miserable trip, and I opened the front door and felt the silence coming from my mother's room, like a presence. It wasn't welcoming or forbidding, just there—sadder and more complete than before, as if suddenly I belonged in it, too.

Instead of telling my mother I will miss her, I can only say, "You're leaving tomorrow."

And instead of saying she'll miss me, too, she says, "Airports," with a little sniff. Then she slumps back in her chair and says, "That was yummy," even though she ate about two bites.

When she takes out a cigarette and book of matches from her pockets, I don't say anything about not smoking in the house. She puts a cigarette in her mouth, gums it thoughtfully. And she doesn't protest when I take the matches gently from her hands, so blue and luminous and small. I strike one, and hold it while she leans in close.

Poison

On Cathy's first day at work, Janice tells her: "I never had an assistant before. I must be moving up in the world." Janice is old enough to be her mother. By ten o'clock, Cathy knows that Janice lost 150 pounds through Jenny Craig, that she uses Auburn Sunset on her hair—which is naturally salt-and-pepper—that her ex-husband is an alcoholic and her current one drives a truck and is gone six weeks at a time. She knows that Janice has one son, Davey, aged thirty, who's a bartender on the east side of town, and that Janice's neighbors throw each other against the wall late at night. Cathy thinks this is Getting Acquainted chitchat, and so tells Janice that she's thinking of going back to school, she's not sure for what yet, and that her job before this one was working at a Mexican restaurant, the same chain she'd worked for back east. She tells Janice that she moved to Tucson from Philadelphia two months ago, that her father lives there still, and that her mother is dead.

After revealing this information, she feels oddly drained and wobbly, transparent, like a jellyfish. She realizes she's shaking. She's not sure why she lied about her mother, but there doesn't seem to be any graceful way of taking it back. ("Oh, did I say *dead*? I meant, in Philadelphia. Sometimes I get them confused, heh heh.") No, there's no way she can change her story now, not after Janice says, "Oh, honey, I'm so sorry. What happened? Do you mind me asking?" And Cathy says quietly, "A car accident. Two years ago," and their small office seems suddenly to be floating like a little boat in the big, gray, scary world.

%

Cathy's mother calls to report that Cathy's father is parked outside her apartment, watching her window.

"I'm going to have to call the police," her mother says.

"It's not like he's dangerous or anything. I mean, he's not threatening you."

"You think watching my window all night isn't threatening?"

Cathy sighs and moves the phone on her shoulder. The television is going—footage of the monsoons, of cars bobbing in muddy, rushing water. She'd expected Tucson to be dry and hot, like deserts are supposed to be; the rain seems like betrayal.

"He would never hurt you is what I'm saying. He's just having a hard time getting used to the fact that you actually left him. Don't make it worse." A photograph of a woman's face appears on the television screen, smiley and washed out. Cathy puts the phone down and turns up the volume, hears a newscaster say there has been a drowning. When Cathy picks up the phone again her mother is saying, ". . . ways of hurting people that don't involve actually physically harming them."

"I have to get off the phone," says Cathy. "There's lightning." She hangs up fast, as if her life depends upon it.

%

Their office is across the hall from the lab, where scientists in sanitary outfits that look like bunny suits bustle in and out all day. Cathy sits at the desk against the wall and when the phone rings she picks it up and says, "Garrett Labs, Cathy speaking," in a friendly, helpful voice, then transfers the caller—"Please hold!"—to the lab or to some other office. Sometimes she hits the wrong button and the person calls back, annoyed. "These phones are a pain in the butt," Janice told her. "I'm always losing people, too." Their office is part of an engineering center that tests silicon wafers. Cathy isn't clear on how this is done, but it has something to do with poisonous, explosive gases that are employed in helpful, useful ways. "We don't have to know what goes on in there, " Janice told her. "What we don't know won't hurt us."

Cathy isn't sure why Janice thinks she needs a full-time assistant. The tasks she is actually assigned—typing envelopes, making up labels for files—Cathy completes in less than an hour, though she tries to space things out—by taking twenty minutes to type a label, for instance, or a half hour to copy ten pages. Mostly, though, Janice sits at her desk, holding a manila folder, and Cathy sits at hers, also holding a folder, sometimes pretending to be interested in its contents, shuffling the pages around importantly—or just resting her fingers on the typewriter keys, as if she's actually in the middle of doing something—and Janice talks. After a month, Cathy understands that her job, what she is being paid $6.50 an hour for, is to reassure Janice that her life is no worse than anyone else's, that she is not strange or depraved. Cathy is not so sure.

In a way, this is the most exhausting job she's ever had—keeping track of what happened when (there were the abused-wife years in Oklahoma, the Jehovah's Witness years, the move to Tucson, the remarriage), and then asking questions that are pertinent but not prying.

"Could you tell it by looking at me?" Janice says, after she's been talking for a half hour about how she used to go door to door, trying to save people. "I mean, I don't look like your typical religious fanatic, do I?"

"You don't look like any kind of fanatic," Cathy says, and is pleased to see Janice smile gratefully.

"You say all the right things," Janice tells her.

%

Cathy shows Janice a picture of herself and her parents at the beach the summer she was sixteen. In the picture, which her father took with a timer, they are kneeling in the sand with their faces squashed close together. Cathy is in the middle and her parents both have their eyes squeezed shut. The rim of her father's blue sun visor is rammed into Cathy's cheek.

"What a cute family!" says Janice. "You look just like your mother."

This is a lie—everyone's always told Cathy she looks like her father, and she does: dark hair, Irish face, long limbs. "And she's a knockout, too." Another lie. In the picture, her mother just looks puffy and sunburned. For most of Cathy's life, her mother was overweight and looked older than she was—people mistook her for Cathy's grandmother—but lately she's informed Cathy that she's lost ten pounds, dyed her hair strawberry blonde, and started wearing shorter shirts and higher heels, to show off what she calls her "gams."

The trip to the beach was Dr. Fuller's idea. Dr. Fuller was their shrink. Dr. Fuller was Cathy's mother's idea. They all three saw him together and separately, and during Cathy's sessions she tried to fake various psychotic disorders. She'd read somewhere that people with multiple personalities close their eyes and droop their heads when a new personality is about to take over. She did this once, and opened her eyes to find Dr. Fuller frowning at her. "Isn't there anything you want to talk about?" he said.

"Oh, I'm sorry," she said brightly. "Were you talking to me?"

Other times she took a magazine and read it for the whole forty-five minutes. When she told her parents this, her mother had muttered something about wasting time and money and her father had said, "Really, Cathy," but after her mother left the room he laughed and patted her on the back. She felt a twinge of glee, as if the two of them were in cahoots.

"What do you tell him?" she asked.

"Oh." Her father shrugged. "Whatever he wants to hear, I guess."

Dr. Fuller said it was important for them to get away together to a new environment, where they could relax and enjoy one another's company without the intrusion of daily stressors. "Has everybody remembered to bring their daily stressors?" Cathy's father asked when they were in the car. "Because I'm not going back!"

"I think," said Cathy's mother, "the point was *not* to bring them."

"Can't Dad make a joke?" said Cathy.

"I suppose," said her mother.

They relaxed and enjoyed each other's company for about two days. Later, in Dr. Fuller's office, he asked them to each give their interpretation of what happened. "He refuses to discuss things," said her mother. "If there's any kind of conflict, he just stomps off—which makes *me* mad, when I might not have been mad before. And then what could have been a simple discussion about whether we go to a movie or not turns into a big, ugly production."

"Somebody slipped a daily stressor into my soup," was all her father said.

He didn't know that, when he'd slammed out of the motel, Cathy's mother had locked herself in the bathroom to cry, or that Cathy had followed him down the beach, trailing at a distance, watching him stomp over the sand. He didn't know that she had seen him walk into the ocean, fully clothed, up to his armpits, and that she'd felt a sudden pang of fear, as if he might keep on walking. Did fathers drown themselves? She looked up and down the beach, to see if there was someone she could call to help him. And then he turned around and splashed back to the shore, and Cathy ran back to the motel, where her mother was still in the bathroom, running the faucets.

"Cathy?" said Dr. Fuller. "What do you think happened?"

"I'm afraid I don't know," she told him sweetly. "I was reading a magazine."

That was the last time they all went to see Dr. Fuller. It was also the last time they went on vacation.

"Right after that picture was taken," Cathy tells Janice, "I nearly drowned." She's aware of wanting to be caught, of wanting Janice to say she doesn't believe a word of it. Janice is leaning forward with her elbows on the desk. Cathy feels her heart pounding, her face getting warm. "I was stung by a jellyfish first, which made me sort of woozy, and then *blam*. Wiped out by a wave."

"Who saved you?" Janice chews briefly on her pinky nail, like a child.

"My dad." Cathy picks the picture up, holds it out in front of her as if she's farsighted. "See that hat? He lost it."

%

The mother who had died had been cremated and sprinkled by Cathy herself over Lake Placida, in Bloomington, Indiana. Cathy isn't sure if Bloomington, Indiana, even has lakes, but she knows Janice has never been there and won't know the difference. It was dusk, Cathy said. A humid, June night at dusk. Cathy and her father took a ferry across Lake Placida, and she held the little urn in her hands, and there were gulls calling and swooping. Were there gulls in Indiana? "And blue herons," she adds quickly. "My father proposed to my mother by that lake, and he said there were herons then, too."

The actual proposal, she knows, had taken place in her father's dorm room at Indiana State. Lately, her father has been talking about this with increasing frequency and wistfulness, reconstructing the events of that night as if he were trying to solve a crime. "It was a Tuesday," he said. "At least I think it was, or maybe Thursday? Ah, shit." Was it before dinner or after dinner? "But she did say yes right away, I remember that much."

"She said yes right away," Cathy tells Janice.

"Your poor father," Janice says, concern pinching her face. "How is he doing?"

"Oh, he's doing really great, actually. I mean, he misses my mother and all, but he's getting on with things. He's dating this really sweet woman. I hope they get married someday."

"He sounds like someone who deserves to be happy."

"He thinks so," Cathy says.

%

"You should date or something," Cathy tells her father.

"How can I? I can't ever trust anyone again."

"Not everyone's going to leave you."

"How do I know that?"

"How do you know you're not going to get smashed by a truck tomorrow morning when you step out the front door? But you'll step out the front door anyway."

"Who knows?" says her father grimly. "Maybe I won't."

%

Every Thursday at one, Cathy unlocks the lab so a man named Ben in an orange jumper can wheel in the weekly supply of nitrogen—big gray tanks, like dirty snowmen with valves for heads. Ben hangs around outside the office, telling Janice and Cathy about his near-death experiences in a pleasant, throaty voice, reeling off the lists of possible ways to die. If the wrong chemicals get mixed together, if there are leaks in the tanks. "There are gases that'll kill you before you even smell 'em," he tells her, leaning his orange shoulder against the door frame. "There are ones that'll destroy your liver first, then your brain. There's ones that by the time you start to feel sick—" he snaps his fingers. He tells her about people he knew who'd been blown up or asphyxiated.

There's something strangely thrilling about working in a place so potentially deadly. Janice isn't concerned. "I've worked here for six years," she's told Cathy, "and nothing's blown up yet." She says this wistfully, as if she wishes something would.

%

In Pennsylvania, Cathy lived an hour and a half away from her parents, who had visited her twice in two years: once just after she'd moved in, and once on her birthday, to deliver a chocolate ice cream cake. On the night her mother moved out, Cathy's father showed up at her door, crying and telling her, "You knew she would do this. You knew and you didn't warn me!"

He looked wilted, like a dog in the rain. His shoulders sagged under his blue windbreaker. He looked like somebody she'd never seen before, and for a moment Cathy considered closing the door on him.

"I didn't," she lied, and let him in.

Her mother had called her the night before and Cathy had said, "You gotta do what you gotta do, I guess."

"I gave him plenty of time to shape up," said her mother. "He won't go see Dr. Fuller, he won't sit down and discuss the things that need discussing. He doesn't care that I feel neglected." She said this accusingly, as if Cathy were somehow to blame.

"Well," said Cathy. "Where are you going?"

Cathy's mother gave her the name of an apartment complex in the city. She gave Cathy her new phone number and said, "Are you writing this down?"

"Yes," said Cathy, not writing.

Cathy's father stood looking around her apartment as if he didn't know whether he was allowed to sit down. "Sit anywhere," she told him, and he sank onto the sofa with a sigh that was almost a groan. He leaned forward and sobbed into his hands and Cathy felt something in her stomach give way, like a building falling down. She had never seen her father cry before.

"Just," she said helplessly. "Just stay here for a while. Lie down."

"Your mother," he said, and swung his feet onto the sofa, slammed his head down on the armrest at the other end. He winced. He had his arm up in the air, the joint of his elbow shielding his eyes.

Cathy didn't know what to do. "Here," she said, and went off to her room to get a blanket and a pillow.

"Thanks." Her father lifted his head so she could put the pillow underneath. His sadness was like something rushing toward her, and she stepped back from the sofa.

"I'll let you sleep," she said, and left him there. She heard him leave early in the morning, before dawn. On the back of the sofa, on top of the pillow and the folded blanket, he left her a note on a napkin—*I don't know what I would do without you.*

That day, she put an ad in the paper to sell her car, her futon, her CD player. She asked her boss at the Mexican restaurant if he knew of any other openings, at any other chains, anywhere else. When her mother called to ask Cathy how her father was holding up and if she had been to see him, Cathy said he was a grown man, he could take care of himself.

%

It happens, finally: a tank starts to leak and they have to evacuate the building. It isn't as dramatic as Cathy expected a thing like that to be; the lab workers simply come walking out the orange doors across the hall and one of them says, "You guys might want to come outside for a minute until we figure out what-all's going on in there."

It rained last night but you can't tell now, except for the pieces of shaggy palm tree lying like wreckage on the pavement. The heat is like something with hands; Cathy can feel it around her neck and on the top of her head and the backs of her legs. This was the sort of thing she'd expected—a sun that bore down on her like a beam from a spaceship; a dried-out world. To the north, the Catalina Mountains are hazy blue lumps.

"And everybody stands two feet from the door," says Janice. "Like that's going to do us any good if the place blows sky-high."

"It won't though, will it?" says Cathy.

"We can hope." Janice looks around. "I want to smoke," she announces suddenly. "Seems like a shame to waste all this fresh air. Not that it's exactly fresh," she adds, wiping the back of her hand across her damp forehead. "Don't you miss normal weather?"

"Sometimes," Cathy admits. She's been telling her father about the desert, describing the mountains and the cactus and the stars, lying about the heat being not so bad. "You should come visit me," she tells him, and he mumbles about being broke, about not having the energy to go anywhere. "Snap out of it!" she told him once, and he'd just sighed. "I've snapped all right," he said.

Janice pats Cathy on the shoulder. "Don't look so scared."

"I'm not!" Cathy laughs. "I'm just hot is all." She flaps her hand at her face, uselessly.

"We should just go home," Janice says, but they are already being waved back inside. They file in behind the lab workers and the other secretaries in their spiky heels, everyone groaning like schoolchildren after a fire drill.

When Cathy's father calls that night to tell her how sad he is and how badly he misses her mother, she lets him talk for a few minutes and then says, "I'm sorry to interrupt you, Dad, but I just want you to know one of the tanks across the hall started leaking poisonous gases today. It exploded. I'm lucky to be alive."

There's a stunned silence. "Geez, Cathy. Are you all right? Was anybody hurt?"

"I'm fine. The woman I work with, though, she got hit by some glass and might have permanent eye damage."

"Geez, Cathy. You've gotta get out of there. Find a new job."

"I'm lucky to have this one," she says. "It's hard to find anything out here."

"I wish I could send you some money." She detects a degree of whiney-ness creeping into his voice, the way it does when he's talking about her mother. "If your mother hadn't left me, my business wouldn't be failing and I could help you out."

"Well, anyway," says Cathy cheerfully. "I guess things are just bad all over."

%

When Arnold, Janice's husband, is home, she comes to work late and leaves early and takes days off, telling Cathy, "If you absolutely *must* call me at home—don't!"

Cathy sits at Janice's desk, which is bigger than hers and faces the hallway, and when people pass by they say, "Looking good, Janice. You lose some weight?" Sometimes, when no one's around, Cathy reads magazines, or snoops through Janice's desk. She feels furtive doing this, but she tells herself she might as well be looking for a key or a pen. She isn't actually sure what she *is* looking for—it isn't as if Janice can possibly have any secrets. But there's something oddly comforting about rooting around, finding Janice's makeup mirrors and Tic Tacs and stale pieces of Big Red and nail files: tiny mundanities floating around in all that drama and heartbreak.

After Arnold's visits, Janice always has a whole slew of new stories to tell Cathy, so that for the first day or two after she comes back they get literally nothing done—answering and transferring the phones when necessary, but not even making a pretense about holding folders or typing anything.

Usually Janice reports their sexual escapades first, and then goes on to the smaller, daily events—what she fixed Arnold that he wouldn't eat, the way he complained about his stiff knees, the stupid movie he'd rented and made her watch. Cathy has figured out that her responses are to be mainly nodding and smiling and leaning forward in her chair, but sometimes she's expected to provide feedback—to tell Janice that she's sure Arnold didn't mean to be a jerk when he wouldn't take her out to dinner because he wanted to stay home and watch television, or maybe that he in fact *is* a jerk and that Janice can do better. She watches Janice's face for clues to what her reaction should be. If she's looking sad and saying, "I deserve better than an idiot, don't I?" Cathy nods vigorously and assures her that she not only deserves better, she could probably find somebody wonderful with no trouble whatsoever. Or if she seems wistful and says something like, "Arnie's a good guy—I mean, nobody's perfect, and marriage is about more than going out to dinner," Cathy will say she's sure they'll work everything out.

One day Janice actually bursts into tears right there at her desk, when she's telling Cathy about Arnold refusing to give up truck driving and get a job in Tucson.

"I know I should trust him, you know? But he's out there on the road all the time, and I've seen some of those floozies who hang around truck stops." Her shoulders sag forward. She puts her face in her hands.

Cathy gets up from her desk and goes around to Janice's chair, stoops down and hugs her around the neck. She smells like floral soap.

"Oh thank you, I needed that." Janice pats Cathy's fingers. "I'm sorry I'm blubbering like an idiot." Then she lifts her head, and Cathy almost topples backwards. "Things were pretty good with your parents, weren't they? I mean, there was none of this kind of shit going on."

"Things were pretty okay," Cathy says, and Janice pats her fingers again and tells her she's lucky.

%

"I just want you to know," says Cathy's mother, "that I would understand if you don't want to come home." She's just told Cathy that her father is in the hospital, that he tried to kill himself in his car while he was parked outside her apartment. "The doctors seem to think it was more of an attention-getting thing. He didn't even have the hose hooked up right, and you know your father—he's very mechanically oriented. He wouldn't get a thing like that wrong unless he meant to."

Cathy's father says: "So now I'm certified loony!" He sounds cheerful. "Your old dad's got a screw loose, I'm not playing with a full deck. What's another one? Out of my tree or something. Off my rocker."

"Why did you do it?" says Cathy. "What were you thinking?"

"I was thinking," says her father, "that I couldn't bear to be in that house without your mother. It's like I'm dying in there. So I just thought—hell. She wanted to be rid of me, now she'll be rid of me."

"She didn't want you *dead*," says Cathy. "Nobody wants you dead."

"Well," he says. He doesn't sound cheery anymore. "I know. But I screwed up anyway, like I screw everything up."

Cathy can't think of anything to say. In the silence, she hears something like a television going, and laughing that sounds like it doesn't come from the TV.

"Who's in your room?"

"I'm in the dayroom. There's all kinds of crazies here."

"You're not a crazy," Cathy tells him.

"Oh, I'll be all right. Hey, whatever happened to that lady with the glass in her eye? The one who was hurt in the explosion?"

"You know what?" says Cathy. "She's doing great. She can see perfectly. And the company even gave her all this money, so she wouldn't sue them I guess, and now she and her husband are buying a house."

"I'm glad to hear that. I worry about you, though. I wish you'd find a safer job."

"I might have actually found one," she tells him. "Things are looking up."

⁂

When Cathy tells Janice that her father's getting married, Janice jumps out of her chair and throws her arms around Cathy's neck.

"You just take as much time off as you need," Janice says. "I'll get some weirdo temp in here and talk her ear off while you're away."

Janice buzzes the lab and tells them she has to drive Cathy home—"She's barfing in here!"—and then they go to a bar to celebrate.

"They'll have to come out here and visit," Janice says when they're settled on barstools. They're the only people there. The bartender slaps down two napkins and Janice orders two whiskey sours. "Where are they going for their honeymoon?"

"Paris."

"Paris! Oh, no, let me," Janice says, going for her purse. "It's my indirect wedding present to your father—getting his little girl sloshed in the middle of the day." She slides a whiskey sour over to Cathy. "I adore these things," Janice says. "I could drink them all day." She nudges Cathy with her elbow. "And maybe we will. Cheers!" They clink glasses. "To your father's new life."

"Here here," says Cathy, and takes a sip. She doesn't like whiskey, but she likes that she's here in a bar in the early afternoon, getting drunk with Janice. Sometimes they'd joked about sneaking a flask of something into the office, and she imagines that if they did, they would probably talk about the same sort of things, and do the same amount of work.

Janice is telling her again about the ways Arnold annoys her. "He gallivants around buck naked, which I cannot *stand*—I mean, how do you talk to somebody when his private parts are all flapping in the breeze?"

"Ha!" Cathy lets Janice buy her another whiskey sour. They aren't bad, if you drink them fast. Janice talks more about Arnold, and about the house she wants to buy if he'll ever quit truck driving and stay in one place. She tells Cathy about Arnold's son, Bobby, from his first marriage, and how he lives with his screwy mother in Texas and is spoiled rotten and wants to come visit them in Tucson—"When hell freezes over," Janice says huffily—and then she orders another round of whiskey sours. "You like these, don't you?"

"I can take 'em or leave 'em," Cathy says, grinning. "But I think I'll take 'em."

"There's this whole other side of you coming out." Janice leans back on her barstool and stares at Cathy as if she's never seen her before. "We'll have to go out to happy hour sometime when you get back. And you had better come back."

"Oh," says Cathy. "I'll come back." She sips her drink through the stirrer. She has no idea if she's coming back. Her mother sent her a round-trip plane ticket but she doesn't know if she'll use it, or if she'll change it, or if she'll sell it. She imagines her mother waiting for her at the airport, watching the passengers file off the plane, none of them Cathy. She's feeling drunk and dopey and wants suddenly to confess, to cry and cry and let Janice tell her everything will be all right, that things are not so awful; she wants to hear again about how terrible things were in Oklahoma, how life was hard but now it's better; she wants to hear that everything works out for the best. She opens her mouth but all that comes out of it is a sigh. Janice reaches over and pats Cathy on the back of her hand.

"I'm so happy about your dad." She looks at Cathy, her eyes alight with something like gratefulness. "We all deserve to be happy, don't we?" she says, and all Cathy can do is nod and say yes, yes, we certainly do.

Strange Weather

The country singer was in the driveway again, her miniskirt bunched around her waist, screaming for Thea's daddy. His name was William but she was crying for Billy, which is what he was called back when they dated each other. She leaned over Thea's mother's Nissan Sentra, shaky in her high heels, and just stayed that way, her thong-clad bottom glowing in the moonlight. Was she kissing the car's hood?

Thea's mother said, "I hate to call the police on her." They were standing at the open kitchen window, Thea with her face close to the screen and her mother with one arm crossed over the other, frowning. Thea's mother had married William nineteen years ago; that's how long it had been since he'd dated the country singer. But apparently she'd never forgotten about him.

It was ten-thirty at night, the moon full in the late-September Tennessee sky. Before the ruckus on the lawn, Thea had been staring out her bedroom window, watching the moon get higher, shrinking and brightening. At midnight, she was going to leave through that window and run down the gravel driveway to the main road, where her boyfriend, Deloye, would be waiting for her on his Honda Scooter. She'd get on the back, grab hold of his waist, and they'd drive the fourteen miles to Nashville. She didn't know what they'd do there. The one time she'd been with her parents, they had gone to the Country Music Hall of Fame. Thea didn't think much of country music.

"What are you going to do?" she asked her mother. By then the country singer had raised her face to the moon—Thea thought she might howl—and seemed to be praying. She staggered away from Thea's mother's car and back to her own—a black convertible of some kind—and got in. Thea could hear her cussing as she fumbled with her keys. The engine started up and then the country singer squealed out of their yard.

This was the third time in a month she'd shown up like this.

Thea's mother closed the curtain. "Go to bed," she said to Thea.

"What if she gets into an accident and gets killed? What if she kills somebody else? She's obviously —" Thea almost said *fucked up*. "She's obviously drunk."

Thea was almost sixteen years old, but her parents still got mad at her for cussing, even though they did it all the time. Or they used to—back when they weren't pretending to be a happy couple. Before her father started coming home every night with lame presents that made her mother say, "Well, thank you very much. How very nice."

"Go to bed," said her mother now.

Thea went to her room and sat in the dark. The whole house seemed to be holding its breath, and she thought she could hear wild animals creeping out of the woods, rustling beneath her window. There was the sound of scratching from under the house—squirrels, probably, or cats. The moon had become hard and glinting. There was no way she could sneak out of the house tonight, and it was all the country singer's fault. She thought of sending Deloye a quick text message, telling him not to bother coming, but he was already on his way to her, speeding over the gravel roads. Unless he met the country singer coming the opposite direction, and she killed him with her black convertible.

As soon as Thea thought this, she knew it had happened; she lay awake in her clothes, trying hard to cry for the boy she had loved, who had been taken from her. The harder she tried to cry, the more she forgot what his face looked like, and she thought that was probably not how it was supposed to be.

%

The next morning, eating her cornflakes, Thea wondered if it had all been a dream—not just last night, but the past six months: her father moving to Seattle without them, the two weeks she spent in the hospital after the cat bit her, her parents getting back together, the move from Jackson, Mississippi, to Tennessee. If she closed her eyes, she could be back in the house in Jackson where she had grown up, where she and her mother had planted hot peppers in the back yard.

"Open your eyes. You're dribbling milk," her mother said. "Do you have your umbrella?"

Outside, the sky was damp and dripping, the yard filling up with mud puddles where the country singer had driven across it.

"My umbrella's somewhere," said Thea. "Are you going to tell Daddy about last night?"

Her mother was standing by the kitchen window again, like she had the night before, arms crossed. She was wearing red terry-cloth sweatpants that revealed the dimples in her butt. Thea resented her mother for her dimpled-butt genes, which she knew she had inherited, and for her tendency to stand in one place and scowl before answering a question.

"Your father will want to know why there are tire tracks all over the yard," her mother said at last, which didn't entirely answer the question.

Thea thought of asking why they had moved to Tennessee in the first place if her father was going to be gone half the time to company headquarters in Seattle anyway. He was a semiconductor engineer, whatever that meant, and he had moved them all back to his hometown so he could "reconnect with the family." Which meant Thea and her mother, seeing as his parents were both dead. Thea would have rather moved to Seattle, but when she mentioned this, her father had told her it wasn't up for discussion.

"She creamed your flower bed," Thea said to her mother.

%

Thea was at her locker when she saw Deloye approaching out of the corner of her eye. She wondered if she might faint; her heartbeat was in her throat. She opened her mouth to get enough air. Then he was beside her, smelling like stale cigarette smoke, and all he said was, "Hey, sorry I couldn't make it last night."

"What?" she said, the spell breaking, her pulse returning to sluggish normality.

"Yeah, I guess I lost track of time."

"Okay," she said.

Deloye was a chubby, curly-haired boy in muddy shoes. She felt herself blushing. Who had she lain awake half the night wishing for?

"It's okay," she said again.

"Catch you next time," he said.

%

Thea's father arrived home in time for dinner, bearing chicken in a cardboard bucket, holding it aloft like it was the Holy Grail. He kissed Thea's mother on the lips like a character in a movie, lingering a little too long, touching her face, staring into her eyes. To Thea he said, "Homework?"

"No," she said automatically, the lie so obvious yet so insignificant that no one thought to question it.

"How was your trip?" her mother asked, holding a chicken leg daintily, as if it were a teacup.

"Fine!" he boomed. Her father tended to boom one-word answers when there was something he didn't want to talk about, then follow up with a loud, desperate chuckle. He did this now, then tore off a piece of chicken breast with his teeth. There was something fierce and violent about the way he chewed; Thea suddenly found herself wondering if he'd ever eaten dinner with the country singer. It was a thought that made her throat close up a little, and she coughed. She knew they must have kissed, maybe even did more than that. (She'd never asked, of course.) But the thought of them sitting across from each other, eating dinner—maybe in a nice restaurant? Why did that seem so disturbing and impossible? He had taken Thea out to a fancy restaurant once when she visited him in Seattle, a dimly lit seafood establishment with candles on the tables. Thea had felt mortified, convinced that the other diners thought her father was a perv on a date with a teenager—a bald, overweight perv who had to find a date over the Internet with a minor.

"She was here again," Thea's mother said. "If you're wondering what happened to the lawn. You really ought to talk to her, or get a restraining order. Or something."

Thea's father hadn't been home the other times the country singer had shown up. She probably didn't know he had gotten fat and bald. She definitely didn't know he tweezed the hairs in his nose, leaving what looked like gray and brown splinters in the bathroom sink. Would she want her Billy if she knew all that? Thea doubted it.

"She's harmless," her father said. "But if she comes back, I'll talk to her. If I'm not here, then call the police." He smiled at Thea. "Enjoying your chicken?"

"Sure," she said.

"It's very nice," said her mother, her eyes fixed on a wing. "Thank you."

%

Thea's friend Leanne said, "I've heard of her! She was big in the eighties. I think my parents have her records. Not CDs, either—*records*."

It was Saturday afternoon. They were sitting in Leanne's basement, which was decorated with pictures of a well-known family of country singers. Leanne's mother was an entertainment lawyer and often went on tour with the family; she was in charge of keeping the mother and the oldest daughter from ripping each other's throats out, mainly by taking them to Denny's and buying them coffee until they sobered up.

"I looked for her songs on iTunes," Thea said. "But they weren't there."

Leanne was on her knees, rummaging through a big cardboard box of albums. If anyone had the country singer's records, it would be Leanne's parents. They also had a record player.

"This is the one I've heard of," Leanne said. "*Blood Orchid*, it's called."

Leanne handed Thea the album, which featured the country singer—blonde and red-lipped—sitting on a rickety-looking front porch with a guitar. She was wearing a tank top and a prairie skirt and pointy-toed boots. She was smiling. Thea had never seen the country singer smile in real life; it made her look like someone else entirely.

"Put it on," said Thea.

Leanne took the record out of its sleeve and blew on it. She placed it on the turntable, flipped some switches. The stereo crackled.

Then the country singer was singing about wild orchids that die when you touch them—*The heat of my hands, it proved too much. Your bruises were there, long before we touched.*

"I don't get it," said Leanne. "She bruised a flower?"

"Shh," said Thea. She didn't get it, either, but the country singer's voice she almost got, the way it sounded both sweet and broken, like shards of moonlight.

She and Leanne sat there on the floor, leaning back on their arms until they got stiff and numb. When it was time to flip the record over, Thea did it herself. Every once in a while Leanne would say, "What the?" but Thea ignored her. There were no lyrics on the record sleeve, so she had to listen carefully to see if there was anyone named Billy in any of the songs. Leanne gave a loud, obnoxious sigh and went upstairs.

After *Blood Orchid* was over, Thea put on *Strange Weather* and *Crack My Heart*, and finally Leanne's mother came downstairs and asked if she wanted to stay for dinner.

"No, thank you," Thea said. She stood up, feeling dizzy. When she walked the four blocks home, it was starting to rain. Damp leaves stuck to her shoes. The waning moon was rising behind the red brick houses of her neighborhood. The rain came harder, and she slowed down. She took off her jacket and let the rain slap coldly against her bare arms, and by the time she got home she was drenched and shivering.

"What happened to you?" her mother cried. The house was bright and smelled like macaroni and cheese.

"Nothing!" Thea said, her own voice sounding peculiar and hoarse.

"I hope you don't catch cold. I'll run you a bath. Why didn't you call for me to come pick you up?"

"I could not speak, and the rain came down, hard as a feather," Thea murmured. Her mother stared at her. "I ran for my life, in the strange, strange weather."

Her mother frowned. "I hope you don't catch cold," she said again.

%

On her cell phone, Thea carefully typed out a message:

Dear Deloye,
You have cracked my heart open. When I think of how we never touched, how I never got the chance to heal your bruises, I feel myself bleeding like a flower.
Althea

A few minutes later her phone beeped. There was a message from Deloye:

Wtf? U ok? C u l8r.

"Well, shit," said Thea.

%

The next day, when her father was watching football with a big bowl of nachos resting on his stomach, Thea perched on the edge of the sofa and said, "Why did you break up?"

Her father put a chip into his mouth and chewed very loudly. He swallowed, then said, "We were fighting a lot, remember? And we didn't actually break up, Thea. We just took some time apart, that's all."

She had meant why did he and the country singer break up.

"What were you fighting about?"

She knew all about Flicka, because her mother had told her. Flicka wasn't her real name; she was her father's secretary ("Such a cliché," her mother had sighed) and she had a horse-face. Even Thea's father called her Flicka. Her real name was Peggy.

"None of that matters," her father said, staring at the TV screen. "What matters is that we're back together."

"Why are you back together?"

"Love," her father said, and patted her on the hand.

%

Thea knew that she was the reason her parents were back together. For the first few days at Jackson Memorial last June, when she was drifting in and out of consciousness, she was aware of only three things: her throat was always dry, her arm ached, and her parents were in the same room but not screaming at each other.

"If I'd known it would make you guys like each other again, I would've gotten rabies earlier," she said, a few days later.

"You don't have *rabies*," her mother snapped, as if it was a disgusting sexual disease. "Don't even say that."

"Then why'd I have to get those shots? Why'd my hand swell up and almost fall off? Why do I have an IV drip?"

"You didn't get rabies," her father said.

"Where's Heathen?"

Heathen was the stray cat Thea had been luring for weeks. She had tried tuna fish, hamburger, deli turkey—all placed in a trap she had made with a box and a stick. She would go out every day after school and hide behind the bushes, waiting for Heathen, until finally the smell of leftover salmon patty did the trick. When she opened the box, he bit her and ran away. Thea hadn't said anything to her parents about it, until her hand swelled up and she passed out during gym class.

"Heathen ran away," her father said, but he wasn't looking at her.

A week later, when Thea went home with antibiotics and strict instructions never to touch stray animals, her father announced that he'd gotten transferred to Nashville, near where he'd grown up, and they were moving in three weeks.

Now that they were all living together again, her father still stayed late at work like he used to, coming home cranky at nine or nine-thirty. The difference was that this time he usually brought home presents—Whitman's Samplers, bouquets of daisies or carnations or roses. The house was full of vases of wilting flowers, and Thea's mother was putting on weight. She would sit in the kitchen while Thea's father ate his warmed-up dinner and eat chocolates, leaving piles of brown crinkled wrappers in the trash.

On Tuesday night, the country singer was back again. Thea heard her car squeal into the driveway, heard the car door open and slam. It was eleven-thirty. Thea had just gotten a text message from Deloye: *u up? wat u doin?*

He ignored her during school, except for slamming her locker once and laughing. Leanne said he was a loser, but Leanne had never even been kissed, so what did she know? Thea and Deloye had kissed twice, when he drove her home from school on his scooter. She'd made him park at the end of the driveway so her mother wouldn't see her. It had all seemed very romantic and dangerous, especially since Deloye didn't have an extra helmet for her to wear.

From her bedroom window, Thea watched the country singer stagger out of her car. She was wearing tight jeans and a leather jacket. Her hair was bright red and piled on top of her head, like Pebbles Flintstone. From down the hall, Thea heard scuffling from her parents' bedroom, then her father emerged in a blue flannel robe and sneakers and stormed down the hall and out the kitchen door. She watched him stomp across the gravel of the driveway, watched the country singer turn to him (what would she think of her Billy now?) and open her mouth in something between a chortle and a shriek. Then Thea watched as the woman threw herself into her father's arms—or tried to anyway. Her father wasn't going for it. His arms were crossed tightly over his chest. He said something that

Thea couldn't make out, something that made the country singer take a step backwards and shout, "I *have* a life! Fuck you!"

"Fuck you, too!" her father yelled back.

"You'll *never* be happy," the country singer shouted. Her voice only vaguely resembled the voice on the records: hoarse and broken, but without any sweetness or beauty. She got in her car and squealed out of the driveway. Later, Thea wondered if what she'd said was meant to be a statement or a prophecy.

%

In the morning, Thea said, "What did she want?"

"Who knows?" said her father. He shoveled scrambled eggs into his mouth. He was putting on weight, too. He had taken to wearing khaki pants that were just the slightest bit too tight.

"She won't come back," Thea's mother said. Her eyes were puffy for some reason.

"You know," said Thea, "she hasn't put out an album in eleven years. But her first two won Grammys. I saw a picture of her at an awards show with Madonna. Can you believe that? She met Madonna."

"You don't even like Madonna," her mother said.

"I'll probably be home around ten," her father said. "Don't wait up."

%

The country singer didn't return that week at all. Deloye continued to ignore Thea, and on Friday she saw him talking with some chubby Goth-looking girl outside the art room. Leanne—Thea's only friend—started ignoring her, too, hanging out with Beverly Hoffman, a sophomore cheerleader. Thea pretended she didn't care, and then realized she actually didn't.

Every night for dinner, Thea's mother ordered Chinese food or pizza. She used to be a legal secretary in Jackson, but when they moved to Tennessee she'd said she was going to let Thea's father support her for once. From what Thea could tell, her mother spent all day doing laundry and watching cooking shows. "So why do you keep ordering fast food if you spend all day watching cooking shows?" Thea asked her one evening when they were eating pizza in front of the evening news.

"Don't you like it?" her mother said. "If you don't like it, there's the stove. Cook something."

The house was filling up with flowers and candy; red heart-shaped boxes protruded from the trash cans. Dried-up petals drifted across the carpet, stuck to the bottoms of their shoes.

"You know," said Thea's mother one night, when they had eaten half a bucket of chicken between the two of them. "I wanted to be a novelist, before I married your father. I was very artistic. I had a great imagination. Then I got pregnant." She gave Thea's arm a quick squeeze, as if to say it wasn't her fault.

%

Thea typed on the computer in her father's office:

> *My Darling,*
> *I'm sorry for the way I acted last week. I wish I could be with you. I think about you all the time. You know everything about love, and my wife knows nothing.*
> *Yours,*
> *Billy*

Then she deleted the last sentence. Her father wouldn't say that, because he didn't know anything about love, either. He thought love was candies and flowers; he listened to Jimmy Buffet. But then she retyped it, because maybe that was something Billy would say.

Maybe it would help the country singer to write more songs.

> *P.S. If you want to write a song about me, I don't mind.*
> *xxoo*

The country singer didn't have a Facebook page, but there was a Web site, last updated three years ago, that had a link to a Yahoo address. Thea had set up a Yahoo address in her father's name.

She clicked *Send.*

Her father was allergic to cats, but when he moved to Seattle last spring, leaving Thea and her mother behind in Jackson, there didn't seem to be any reason not to get one—especially when they started coming out of the shrubbery behind the house, flushed out by the bulldozing in the vacant lot across the street. Every other day or so, there would be a kitten smashed in the road; Thea would scoop it up with her shovel and bury it beside the hot pepper plants. There were four little graves when her mother said, "That's enough of burying the dead kittens. I don't want you near them."

"Then let me keep a live one!" Thea said. Her mother had been adamant about that, too, claiming they had diseases and worms.

Then a few weeks went by and no kittens ended up smashed in the road, so one afternoon when the bulldozers were parked silent and empty in the vacant lot—they were building a Walgreens—Thea went across the street to see if there were any strays still around. If she actually brought one home, cleaned it up, had it purring in her lap by the time her mother got home from work—surely then she could keep it.

Thea found two scrawny black-and-white cats trapped in a wire cage that had ANIMAL CONTROL stamped on its side. Thea knew her mother was responsible for this; she was always talking about calling Animal Control. The cats were chewing on the bars. When Thea opened the cage, one cat hissed at her and the other opened its mouth like a water snake but no sound came out. They both shot off into the shrubbery. Thea threw the cage under one of the bulldozers.

She named them Heathen and Mute, and she set her own trap for them—an upside-down Amazon.com box with a stick in it, attached to a string. The following day, she found Mute squashed in the middle of the road. She had a little funeral for him and became more determined to capture Heathen. Each day she moved the box a little closer to her yard. Each day, the piece of hamburger or turkey she'd left inside it was gone, and the box was tipped on its side.

Later, when she was out of the hospital, Thea would demand to know what had happened to Heathen. Had he really run away? Had he? *Had* he? "Or did you *kill* him?" she asked her father one night at dinner, tears dripping into her mashed potatoes.

"No, *I* did," said her mother. She looked furious, but at whom or what Thea wasn't sure. "I shot it with your father's rifle. I left it for the foxes to eat." Then she got up from the table and stomped down the hall, leaving Thea and her father staring at each other across what seemed a suddenly vast distance.

%

A few weeks after the country singer showed up the last time, Thea's father said he had to go to Seattle again. He brought home two gigantic teddy bears, one for Thea and one for her mother, and then took them out to dinner at a fancy Indian restaurant in Nashville. He wore a sports coat with his khakis, and Thea's mother wore a red velour dress. Neither of them said anything about how much makeup Thea was wearing, and her mother let her have a sip of wine.

"By the way, I have a boyfriend," Thea announced, crunching on a *pappadam*, feeling bold. "I think I'm in love." She shivered a little; each word was a shiny, hollow object waiting to be filled.

Her parents looked at her. "I am *in love*," she said again. The words felt true, but somehow separate from Deloye or any boy she knew, and even from herself—like treasures placed carefully around a room where she didn't yet belong.

"We would like to meet this boy," her father said at last. "If you're spending time with him."

"What's his name?" said her mother.

"None of your business," Thea said.

"There's no boy," said her father, matter-of-factly. "If there was, we'd know about it."

"You don't know anything," Thea said, and took another sip of her mother's wine.

%

Thea's grades were suffering—as if they were tiny creatures with hearts that could be broken. "Grades," said Thea, "cannot *suffer*."

"No, but you can," said her father. He was packing his suitcase, folding his khaki pants, putting his toiletries into a baggie. Thea wanted to ask him if he was going to go on a date with a woman while he was in Seattle, then decided she didn't care.

"There are stray cats under the house," Thea said. "Maybe I'll try to catch one. Maybe it'll bite me. If you want me to suffer so much."

That shut her father up for a minute. Then he said, tightly, "I am doing everything I can think of to make you and your mother happy. What else can I do?"

Thea didn't have an answer.

"You have straight D's," said her mother. "I see you working on the computer every night. What are you doing?"

What she was doing was writing love letters to the country singer, from Billy. Billy couldn't believe how his life had turned out; it was obvious that he should have stayed with the country singer—*We were so young, what did we know about love? I was a fool*—but now he was trapped in a loveless marriage with a woman who would die without him. *She's nothing like you. She eats candy all day long and says she used to want to be a novelist but I don't know if I believe her. The only good thing about our marriage is our daughter, who is not technically beautiful but has a deep and knowing soul. One day, she will find the kind of love we used to have, and she will not be an idiot and screw it up.*

Thea started off with the intention of sending the letters, but they always ended up long and rambling and mostly about herself—how smart and wise she was—and she wasn't stupid enough to think the country singer would be fooled.

Thea found an old, used cassette of *Strange Weather* on Amazon and ordered it using her father's credit card, the one he forgot he had and kept in his sock drawer. She listened to the tape at night on her ancient Walkman, which she'd had since she was ten and which her mother had appropriated for her power walks, back when she used to leave the house.

Why had Thea been thinking her father and the country singer ate in fancy restaurants? The songs were all about juke joints, drinking too much, smoking, bleeding, wishing you were dead, throwing yourself in Lake Pontchartrain or the Mississippi River. When she'd listened to the record at Leanne's house, she hadn't caught a lot of the lyrics, but now she caught them all. There wasn't a Billy mentioned specifically, but there was someone whom the country singer loved too much, screwed too much, drank too much with, and wanted to die with.

Maybe, thought Thea, the country singer just felt that way about *everybody*. The thought made her breath catch in her heart. How wonderful would that be?

Thea had tried to fall in love with one of the seniors who had a locker close to hers, but she couldn't manage it. She tried to want to slit her wrists because Deloye was dating the Goth Girl, but she couldn't manage that, either. She knew love was waiting for her, but that room of treasure that didn't belong to her was still sealed up, the doors and shutters locked against her.

It was her parents' fault, for making her as dull as they were. She needed to talk to someone who knew how to suffer.

Darling,
My family will be gone the night of Friday, October 29th.
Please come to me.
Yours always,
Billy

Technically, this was only half true. Her father would still be gone, but her mother would be home and asleep. Lately, Thea's mother had been taking nighttime cold medicine, even when she didn't have a cold. She drifted off to bed around eight-thirty, and got up just before Thea left for school.

On the night of October 29, Thea's mother said, "I should apply for jobs, don't you think?"

"Here?" said Thea. "Or back in Jackson."

"I don't know," said her mother.

They were sitting on the sofa watching a show about a team of doctors who solve mysterious cases. Thea had long since given up on homework. She imagined the country singer would tell her that homework didn't matter. They might go to a juke joint, a down-and-out place where no one would care that Thea was underage. She might start smoking.

Before the doctors solved the case, Thea's mother announced that she was going to bed.

"I'll see you in the morning," Thea said, but there was a part of her that wasn't entirely sure this was true. She thought of her mother waking up to find Thea gone, the flower bed destroyed, tire tracks in the driveway. And for some reason, she couldn't imagine where she, Thea, would be—only that her mother would find herself alone, and wish she had tried a little harder to understand love.

%

Thea was waiting on the front porch, shivering in the damp air, when she heard the car coming. It was quarter to one. She had decided that she'd wait until four before giving up. Maybe, after all, the country singer didn't even check her email.

But now that she was actually coming, Thea allowed herself to consider the possibility that she might be angry. After all, she was expecting Billy. But wouldn't she be pleased, in a way, that Billy's daughter wanted—*needed*—to talk to her? Wouldn't she be flattered?

The lights of the black convertible swung through the trees, the tires crunching on the gravel. As the car got closer, Thea could see that the top of the convertible was up. The car left the gravel, heading right for the house, right for the porch where Thea was sitting, now standing, now backing away. She could just now make out the country singer's pale face. She was staring right at Thea as if she was looking through her, into the house where her Billy was. And then the car stopped, idling there on the lawn. Thea had the feeling she had sometimes in nightmares, when she knew the dream should be over but couldn't wake herself up. And then she was running down the porch steps, her entire body strumming some chord she almost knew. When she leaned breathless through the car's open window, a baggy-eyed woman regarded her warily. Her skirt was bunched up, revealing saggy knees. She wore orange lipstick. There was a slash of puckered flesh between her eyebrows. "Take me with you," Thea whispered, and she caught a whiff of something warm and sour as the country singer leaned toward her, as if for a kiss.

"It's too bad," the woman said slowly, in a low and broken voice, "you got your mama's face."

Later, Thea would not be sure if her mother appeared before or after she called for her (her cry a surprising, mortifying *"Ma!"*) and she would be too embarrassed to ever ask. Her mother seemed taller than usual; how did she have time to put on shoes? Her eyes were bright, flashing; she was wearing her red terry-cloth sweatpants. Her hair—wild, frizzed out, strangely beautiful—glowed in the lights from the country singer's car.

"Get away from there, Thea," her mother said, and Thea backed toward the house. "Go inside!"

From the kitchen window, Thea watched as her mother stalked around to the driver's side of the car and pulled the door open. The country singer, affronted, put one sharp-heeled shoe on the ground but Thea's mother said, "Move over," and, shockingly, the country singer did, into the passenger side. Thea's mother got in, slammed the door, put her hands on the steering wheel.

Thea watched the car lights back up, wind their way down the driveway, and finally vanish behind the trees.

%

When her father returned the next evening, he and Thea's mother disappeared into their bedroom and talked for hours in hushed, urgent voices. Thea wondered if her mother was going to tell him what she'd done to the country singer, tell him that she'd arrived home alone at five-thirty in the morning in a taxi.

Finally, they knocked on Thea's door, where she was watching her tiny portable television with the volume on low, flipping through news stations.

Her father said, "I think we need to move to Seattle. All of us." Thea's mother stood behind him, her arms crossed. There was something terrifying about how still she was. "I think we should have done it a long time ago."

"Okay," said Thea.

Her mother came forward then, her hair smelling like moonlight, her face flushed, and kissed Thea on the top of the head.

"That's bullshit," Leanne said, when Thea informed her that they were moving away because her mother had done something terrible to the country singer. Leanne and Thea weren't talking anymore, but Thea had stopped by her lunch table to say good-bye. Beverly the cheerleader regarded her with awe, her fingers gripping her pastrami sandwich.

"She was really mad," said Thea, "and she didn't come home until almost dawn. What do you think of that?"

"I think," said Leanne, "that Denny's is open all night and that's probably how long it took your mother to sober her up enough to yell at her." She sniffed her apple.

"Well, what do you know?" Thea said, and huffed off, feeling flushed and exhilarated. When she'd asked her mother where she and the country singer had gone, her mother had said, "None of your business." Who knew what a woman—even a woman like her mother—was capable of doing for love?

Still, in case the country singer was not lying dead in a ditch somewhere, Thea sent one more email:

Dear Wrinkle-face,
You are a washed-up no-talent alcoholic with extremely bad body odor. Also, you are an idiot because none of these emails have been written by Billy (which isn't even his name!) but by me, the girl with a face like her mother, which is obviously a better face than yours. Why don't you write a song about THAT?

%

She started her new school in January, when the rains in the Pacific Northwest were turning to snow. Her father took her skiing for the first time in her life. Her mother found a job at a lawyer's office and colored the gray out of her hair. Her father still worked late but was more cheerful on weekends, and stopped with the teddy bears, candy, and flowers. Thea met a sophomore named Dale who took her to the movies and texted her twice a day just to say hi. No matter how hard she tried, she couldn't manage to feel tortured, and she realized she liked it that way. When he met her parents, he pronounced them "neat, pretty cool," and she admitted yes, she supposed they were.

That summer, the rains came every day, and sometimes the sun didn't set until after ten o'clock. There were nights when the rain kept Thea awake, her mind racing toward shadows, and it was on one of these nights that she saw the country singer on a late-late talk show—blonde again, wearing red cowboy boots and talking about rehab. She turned the television off before the country singer could perform her new song—which was not about a teenaged girl or a furious wife or even about throwing herself in a lake because of some man. It was a silly, cheerful number about boys and cars, more pop than country, which Thea had heard on the radio several times and didn't much care for.

Acknowledgments

Thanks to the following publications, in which these stories originally appeared: "Trafalgar" in *The Gettysburg Review*, "Vines" in *Fugue*, "Midnight, Licorice, Shadow" in *Crazyhorse*, "Anthony" in the *Mid-American Review* and in *Surreal South '09*, "Grand Canyon" in *Other Voices*, "Poison" in *The Carolina Quarterly*.

Thanks to my parents, Richard Hagenston and Carolyn Fisher, and my in-laws, Rod and Elaine DeRego, for so much love and encouragement over the years; to Antonya Nelson, Robert Boswell, and Kevin McIlvoy, my wonderful teachers at New Mexico State University; to the places and conferences that inspired stories and friendships: Bread Loaf, Sewanee, Yaddo, and the Summer Literary Seminars in St. Petersburg, Russia. Thanks also to my students and colleagues at Mississippi State University; to Mike Rice and Darlin' Neal; to Joyce McMahon, my first and always-honest reader since second grade; to Kevin Watson and Press 53; and to everyone at Eastern Washington University Press, especially Pamela Holway for her terrific work on this book.

And finally, thanks to my husband, Troy DeRego, for absolutely everything.

About the Author

Photo: Troy DeRego

Becky Hagenston's first collection of stories, *A Gram of Mars*, won Sarabande Books' Mary McCarthy Prize as well as the Great Lakes Colleges Association New Writers Award. Her stories have appeared in the O. Henry anthology, *The Southern Review*, *Mid-American Review*, *The Gettysburg Review*, *Crazyhorse*, and many other journals. She lives in Starkville, Mississippi, where she is an associate professor of English at Mississippi State University.

CPSIA information can be obtained
at www.ICGtesting.com
Printed in the USA
LVOW12s0003290316
481182LV00001B/3/P